THE
HEISENBERG
LEGACY

A SAM REILLY NOVEL

CHRISTOPHER
CARTWRIGHT

Copyright © 2018 by Christopher Cartwright

This book is protected under the copyright laws of the United States of America. Any reproduction or other unauthorized use of the material or artwork herein is prohibited. This book is a work of fiction. Names, characters, places, brands, media and incidents either are used fictitiously. All rights reserved.

PROLOGUE

LUFTWAFFE AIRFIELD, STUTTGART—22 JANUARY 1945

OBERSTLEUTNANT WILHELM GUTWEIN watched as the Borgward B 3000 military truck backed up to the tail end of his aircraft. Once the green canvas covering the tray was removed, he received his first glimpse of the strange metallic device, which had been hurriedly transferred in secret from a laboratory in Haigerloch. The instrument looked to him like an oversized, charcoal-painted American football, with four large steel dorsal fins protruding from its back. The body of it appeared swollen, more like that of an elongated sphere than the cylindrical shape of a traditional bomb. Its weight, being instantly apparent on the flatbed as the truck's suspension settled down hard on its axle.

Gutwein stared at the hideous creation.

Its mere presence made the hairs on the back of his neck stand on end and ice-cold fear freeze his spine. It looked malevolent and pervasive, a monster capable of extinguishing all life within an entire city. The thought was abhorrent to him, yes, but a necessary evil. He'd seen what enemy firebombing had done to Hamburg two years ago. A devastating incendiary device like this was the only solution left to his country. He didn't precisely hate the rest of the world. In fact, he felt mostly indifferent. The simple fact remained that they were at war. No matter how abhorrent the outcome, he'd rather have his adversary's cities destroyed than his own.

A hydraulic hoist whirred and groaned, lifting the device into the underbelly of his aircraft. Gutwein listened to the distinctive sounds, as a mechanic ratcheted the bomb onto its purpose-built cradle. After flying the aircraft for the past two years, he felt an intrinsic connection and relationship with the grand metal bird. As he watched, he imagined he could feel his aircraft respond to this new force for destruction by shuddering under its new burden.

He read through the sheaf of papers, a detailed technical report. At a length of a hundred and forty inches, with a width of eighty, it weighed nine thousand, two hundred and thirty pounds. In real terms, the payload was two thousand pounds greater than his aircraft was designed to carry.

He'd commanded some of the best pilots and most honorable men he'd ever known in the *Luftwaffe*, but his last mission would require only one plane. Gutwein turned to admire the lines of the aircraft he'd had the privilege to fly over the past two years. The sight brought a thin-lipped smile to his face. This was her swansong. Never again would his craft look so beautiful, as it was impossible for her to escape this raid in one piece. He felt a rise of bile in his throat, as he realized with dreaded certainty, that it was just as unlikely that he himself would get out alive. Ignoring the probable and most likely inevitable outcome, as in the hands of fate, he studied his aircraft.

The Deutsche Lufthansa Focke-Wulf 200S Condor was never meant to be a bomber. The designation *Condor* was chosen because, like the bird, the FW-200 had a very long wingspan — 107 feet wingtip to wingtip — to facilitate high-altitude flight. Until two weeks ago, it had been used for the sole purpose of reconnaissance over the Atlantic. It was identical to the original commercial long-range airliner that once flew non-stop from Berlin to New York in 1938. To demonstrate German technical capability, it was fitted with extra fuel tanks and used to perform long-range flights. The machine was re-designated FW-200S with the letter S representing the term, "Specialized."

It was a four-engine monoplane, originally powered by four American 875 horsepower Pratt & Whitney Hornet radial engines and intended to carry 26 passengers in two cabins for up to 1,860 miles. Of course, since the war had started, much of the aircraft had been stripped and replaced in order to produce a military production version.

The American Pratt and Whitney Hornet engines were replaced with the native German Bramo 323 R-2 radial engines, featuring water-menthol power boost of 895 kW for take-off. The fuselage was fitted with a full-length Bola ventral gondola, which added a narrow bomb bay to the airframe, increased defensive armament, and provisions for a total war load of 11,902 pounds spread out over each engine nacelle.

Even after two years of flying her, Gutwein still thought she was stunning. An elegant machine of all-metal, light alloy, flush rivet construction, except for fabric-covered flight-control surfaces and the wing covered with fabric aft of the main spar. All flight control surfaces were manually actuated, though the split flaps were hydraulically actuated. It had taildragger landing gear, all with single wheels. These retracted rearward, allowing the gear to fall open if the power system failed. The aircraft was not pressurized, limiting cruise altitude to 9,800 feet.

To adapt it for wartime service, hardpoints were added to the wings for bombs, and the fuselage was strengthened and extended to create more space. Forward and aft dorsal gun positions were added, in addition to an extended-length version of the Bola ventral gondola typical of World War II German bomber aircraft. To complete its militarization, his aircraft incorporated a bomb bay as well as heavily glazed forward and aft flexible defensive machine gun emplacements.

The entire aircraft had undergone a third and even more striking transformation within the past two weeks. Additional long-range fuel tanks were added. The Bola ventral gondola previously fitted on most bombers was removed, and in its place a custom-built cradle for the device was mounted.

To compensate for the additional weight of the bomb and fuel, all non-essential items were stripped from the Condor. The forward dorsal 19-inch turret with a 7.9mm MG 15 machinegun, 13mm MG 131 machinegun in aft dorsal position, two MG 131 guns in beam positions, one 20mm MG 151/20 cannon in front of the ventral gondola, and one MG 15 in the aft section of the gondola were all removed.

His seven-man crew would be reduced to just three — himself, a copilot and a navigator. He would have liked to bring his bombardier along, too. But the weight restrictions meant that he couldn't risk the additional crew. Too much weight, and they would never reach the American coastline and Germany's last hope, would disappear into the Atlantic. No, he had to lose his bombardier. Either he or his co-pilot could make the final drop. From what he'd been told, there would be little targeting required. The device was so powerful, he merely needed to drop it near the city, and the bomb would do the rest.

Once airborne, if they were spotted by anyone, they would be utterly defenseless. But why would they need it? Where they were headed, no one would be expecting them...

Frowning, the pilot finished reading the report, began re-reading it.

A military adviser of smaller stature, yet superior rank strode through the aircraft hangar, stopping in front of him. "Heil Hitler!" He said, saluting by extending his right arm to neck height, then straightening his hand so that it was parallel to his arm.

Gutwein, returned the salute as a show of loyalty and as compelled by law. Originally, the *Wehrmacht* refused to adopt the Hitler salute, preferring to maintain its own customs. Only after the 1944 plot against Hitler were the military forces of the Third Reich ordered to replace the standard military salute with the "Heil Hitler" salutation.

"*Oberstleutnant* Gutwein. You are confident of the route?"

"Yes, sir."

"And do you believe it is possible to make the delivery?"

"It is possible." Gutwein stared up at the clouds, as though making a private concession to his God. "But it won't be up to me whether I succeed or not."

"Are you shunning your responsibility?" The Officer's voice hardened. "Perhaps I should have someone with more confidence fulfil this obligation."

"No. You misunderstand me. I will gladly perform my duty."

"Then what is it?"

Gutwein lowered his gaze to meet the Officer's eyes directly. "I will either succeed with the mission or do the Fuhrer proud in my death." He made a show of sighing deeply. "What I am saying is even with the additional fuel tanks the margin of error is so fine that success will be entirely dependent on favorable winds. If we have those, I'll deliver the package. If it is anywhere near as destructive as Heisenberg leads us to believe, then the allied forces will have no choice but to accept an unconditional surrender."

The Officer smiled, shook his hand warmly. "Wilhelm Gutwein. Good luck. God speed on your mission, and your return."

He stood at attention. "Thank you, sir. Heil Hitler!"

"Heil Hitler!" his superior returned, spinning on his heel and leaving the area.

Gutwein's return was an irrelevant statement, both men knew it for a lie. If the winds were anything but perfect, he would end up ditching in the sea, where he would never be seen again. Even if he succeeded in his mission, there was only enough fuel for the bomb's delivery.

He was on a one-way ticket to the heart of his enemy.

God and winds willing, Gutwein would drop his payload, but his own homecoming was an unlikely possibility.

Even if he survived, and found a place to land afterward, he would most likely be caught and shot. He wasn't worried about the language, he'd studied at Eton before the war. They'd made him a set of identity papers which were nearly a decade out of date, but even that didn't worry him. It was the necessity to live a life of deception that tormented him. He would be worse than a spy. He would have been the one who brought a nation to its knees by what he'd done, then he'd be forced to integrate with his enemies. That is, if he lived long enough to one day make his way home again, one day in the future.

Gutwein shook his head. He prayed he had enough power to allow him to get his aircraft and the device off the ground.

He wore the crisp uniform of the Luftwaffe and on his sleeve, an insignia displayed a pair of wings over two bands, indicating his rank of Lieutenant Colonel. His blond hair was trimmed neatly and pulled back. He had a well-defined jaw line and light blue eyes that once were full of kindness. That kindness had been replaced by hatred after his family were killed during a British air raid on his hometown of Hamburg almost a year ago.

The bombing was followed by a series of losses. The most recent of which was the loss of Normandy, after the assault two weeks ago by the Western Allies. They launched the largest amphibious invasion in history as they stormed the northern coast of France on the 6th of June 1944. It was the turning point, and the German war office knew it. Plans for the release of a secret weapon under construction were expedited and the strange device now in his bomb bay was the result of that effort.

Tomorrow, he would commence the most significant mission of his life. He hoped it would be the greatest turning point toward a German victory.

His thoughts turned to the strange bomb. Horror, defiance, and vengeance were mingled. If the engineers' calculations were right and he could get his aircraft off the ground tomorrow morning, he would save the Fatherland, and have his revenge.

At 2 a.m. a soldier on the night watch woke him. "It's time, *Oberstleutnant* Gutwein."

Gutwein opened his eyes, surprised to find that he had slept. He stood up and greeted the man with a curt "Thank you," which also served to dismiss the soldier. He quickly donned his starched uniform with pride and stepped outside.

Striding over crushed stone on the way back to his hangar, Gutwein noted with satisfaction that it was a remarkably cold night — even for January.

He rubbed his gloved hands together and breathed out, watching his breath mist. He smiled, as it was a very good omen. Cold air meant dense air. The props on his propeller-driven craft would bite deeper in denser air, thrusting a greater mass of air backwards, which meant more thrust and power. Cold, dense air would also provide more lift, essential for the mission.

It might just make it possible to get his overladen Condor off the ground. Luck, he understood through hard-won knowledge, meant everything in the world.

It was good luck turned to bad that had returned his wife and children to Hamburg at exactly the wrong time. Ursula the sensible and determined, had been given a gift of lamb steaks. Under severe food rationing, she had decided to go home early, to prepare the unexpected feast as a surprise.

She did it for me, he mused, a pang of sadness constricting his heart.

It was the same sort of twisted luck that gave him the responsibility to deliver what the history books would likely record as the most catastrophic invention of the human race. A weapon so destructive that, God forgive him, all civilizations would fear and submit to anyone with such a device. Who would risk such devastation more than once?

Gutwein preferred logic, compromise, and cool reason to war. Ordinarily, a peace-loving man, how did the fates see fit to give this duty to him? The mission was never supposed to be his in the first place.

The experimental Messerschmitt Me 264—Amerika Bomber—was supposed to perform the task of trans-Atlantic flight and bombing raid, but three days ago the aircraft had developed engineering problems. These could be overcome with time, but the Third Reich was adamant that here and now was their last chance of success. Thus, the terrible task had fallen to him and his Condor.

Yet, who better to go than a man who had lost his family?

He dismissed the thought as he reached the makeshift hangar where his Condor had been kept. She was lit up with a series of bright lights. A team of engineers and maintenance workers were going over her, searching for any last detail that might cause her to fail.

Standing by her wingtips, were his two men.

"Good morning, gentlemen." Gutwein greeted his copilot and navigator, disregarding the "Heil Hitler" salute.

Both replied, nearly in unison, "Good morning, sir."

To his navigator, he asked, "Have you seen the weather reports for our intended flight track?"

"Yes," Krause replied, handing him the report. "We'll have a moderate tail wind. It's predicted to ease off once we reach the Atlantic, of course, but it will help."

"Good. Any news of enemy aircraft in the area?"

"No. At this stage we'll have a clean run."

"Excellent." Gutwein turned to his copilot. "Have you checked my calculations based on our approximate weight and total fuel capacity?"

"Yes, sir," Vogel replied.

"And?"

"It will be close, sir. If the winds are favorable, or even if the winds aren't against us, we'll make it. Once we reach our target, there won't be a lot of time to locate a suitable landing site, but that was always going to be the case, wasn't it?"

Gutwein nodded. "All right. We have a mission to complete, gentlemen. Let's not keep our lady waiting."

He glanced at his aircraft.

The Focke-Wulf 200S Condor appeared sad and despondent, like a loyal old dog, who knew her days were numbered. Gutwein felt a sudden loss at the thought. He'd commanded similar aircraft since the start of the war. The Condor had been remarkably reliable and had always gotten him home in one piece. Now she was naked and unadorned, as though she was about to be decommissioned and scrapped.

With his copilot, he ran his hand around her nose and fuselage — shining his flashlight into the dark openings of her ailerons in search of any damage the maintenance crew might have done to her when they divested her of so many of her functions. He continued to the tail, placing a hand on it to physically test its actuators. Both pilots completed their outside inspection of the aircraft. Neither spoke and the cold air now turned solemn, as they inspected their aircraft for her last flight.

Gutwein commenced his start-up procedure and went through the rigorous list of cross-checks. An aeronautical engineer had updated them two days ago in light of the enormous distance they needed to cover. Their lives were expendable, so it wasn't for them that so much effort and diligence had been applied. No. It was for the sake of their payload — the unique, cataclysmic bomb the world had never seen.

Once complete, he placed the flight pad down and faced his copilot. "Are you happy to proceed, Mr. Vogel?"

"Yes, sir."

"Good."

Gutwein turned around and faced his navigator who currently took the cockpit's third, and rearward facing seat, usually reserved for the flight engineer. Having reduced their full crew to just three in order to save weight, Krause was now having to play the role of the flight engineer. He was diligently checking the series of flight gauges that monitored everything from oil pressure, to fuel supplies, and engine temperatures.

"Everything good, Krause?" Gutwein asked.

"Yes, sir. She's right to go."

"All right. I'll close the hatch and we'll be off."

Gutwein took a few steps toward the aft section of the Condor and resolutely closed the main hatch. A glance out the open gangway showed a BMW R75 motorcycle racing toward them.

Taking in a deep breath, he sighed. *What now?*

Its rider brought the motorcycle to a stop and switched off the engine. On his crisp uniform he wore the insignia of an SS Intelligence Officer. The man appeared flustered. "You are *Oberstleutnant* Wilhelm Gutwein?"

"Yes."

"We've just received reports of an aerial raid flying across Southern France."

"Do we know what their target is?"

"No."

Gutwein swore under his breath. "So, the mission's been postponed again, has it?"

The SS Intelligence Officer shook his head. "No. There's too much of a chance they will target Stuttgart. We can't allow the weapon to be destroyed on the ground. It's too important. I'm afraid that's not possible." He handed him a written dispatch. "My orders are to inform you to follow the second route."

"There might not be enough fuel." Gutwein said, taking the paper, ripping open the seal, and scanning the short contents of the order.

"Our flight engineers believe it will be close, but you should still make it," the dispatch rider continued speaking. "Risks have been studied, discussed at length, and a decision made. The Führer had ordered this operation to be carried out immediately."

A mixture of dizziness, dread, and madness made Gutwein abruptly feel faint. With reckless abandon, he said, "The Führer's order will be done. Heil Hitler!" he saluted.

"Heil Hitler!" the SS Officer returned. As an epitaph to the madness of this last-chance mission, it seemed appropriate.

Gutwein taxied his craft to the end of the runway.

He pressed his right pedal to the floor and the Focke-Wulf 200S Condor spun to face into the wind, along the center of runway seven-nine. The easterly wind ran at twenty knots, on a dry and cold morning. The weather was one of the few pieces of good luck they still had going for them. He applied pressure with the balls of his feet until he felt the brakes lock tight and the tires firmly grip the blacktop.

He used his right hand to slowly, carefully move all four throttles to full. Like a big dog on a small lead, the aircraft shuddered and strained to break free. The four Bramo 323 R-2 radial engines increased power until their high-pitched whine nearly drowned out all verbal communication. He kept them there, checking all the gauges remained in their correct ranges.

Vogel nodded, and with a thumb pointing upwards, he shouted, "She looks good."

Gutwein brought the throttles back to idle. "You still happy, Mr. Krause?"

"Sure." Krause replied. Gazing pensively out the port window, he said, "The question is, will she get off the ground?"

Gutwein smiled and slapped his engineer's shoulder. "Have some faith. It might just take every last inch of the runway to do so, but she'll fly."

He'd flown test flights on the aircraft with their designer, Kurt Tank, the original engineer whose design had won the contract by Lufthansa, back in the late 1930s. They'd then worked together to modify the civilian commercial airliner so that she was structurally strengthened and fitted with the

German Bramo 323 R-2 radial engines to replace the American made 875 HP Pratt & Whitney Hornet radial engines. Since then, he'd clocked up nearly ten thousand hours on the long-range aircraft—more than any other person alive. He knew exactly how much she could take.

But would her airframe withstand the additional forces?

He'd calculated her take-off weight himself. Between the extraordinary bomb and additional fuel stored in empty bomb bays coupled to the wing, they were overladen by nearly ten thousand pounds. It would be close, but she'd fly. Safety margins were not an issue on this flight.

"All right, gentlemen, here we go."

Once more, Gutwein used his right hand to gradually move all four throttles back to full. Again, the engines whined, and the entire metal fuselage shuddered. The Condor edged forward despite the wheel brakes locked firmly in place.

When the revolutions had nearly red-lined, Gutwein made a silent prayer. Unable to detain her any longer, Gutwein released the brakes, uncaging the Condor—allowing—no *expecting* the great lady to fly.

The high-pitched drone of the powerful Bramo 323 R-2 radial engines increased in pitch until they howled with the wind attempting to extract every single pound of thrust possible. The three-bladed VDM-Hamilton airscrews spun madly until they disappeared from the leading edge of the wing in a haze of gray. He would need every one of their combined 3576 kilowatts to lift her from the runway.

Initially, the overladen aircraft crept forward. Her movement felt slow, restrained to the ground by earthly forces. She gently began building up speed and momentum until she reveled in the challenge of the impossible task given to her.

Through the windshield Gutwein watched as each 1000 foot marker slipped past. Heart in his throat, the end of the runway rapidly ran forward to greet them. His eyes darted between the instrument panel and the distance markers outside. Her tail naturally lifted, making the craft straight and level. He was given a clear glimpse straight down the runway.

"We just passed the 4000 foot marker," Vogel stated.

"Nearly there, just a little bit more acceleration," Gutwein coolly replied. His eyes glanced at the airspeed. The Condor had reached a sluggish 80 knots.

The nose of the aircraft wanted to lift. Gutwein, refusing her natural aerodynamic desire, strained to keep the yoke pushed forward and her wheels on the ground.

"5000 foot," Vogel said. "Speed: 110 knots."

"We're going to need more than that if we want to clear those trees."

They were approaching the minimum takeoff speed of the Condor under normal conditions. Overladen by nearly ten thousand pounds above its ordinary 50,057 pounds maximum take-off weight, Gutwein knew they needed to reach a speed closer to 130 before he even considered allowing her nose off the ground.

The condor's all metal fuselage shuddered under the intense power demand, begging to be released from the confines of gravity. He needed all the speed he could gather to get the overladen aircraft into the sky and climbing to clear the trees. Gutwein kept the stick all the way forward, trying to keep the nose from lifting.

Not until we're ready, darling, he murmured under his breath.

He looked down again. Their speed had reached 125 knots. Nearly there, they were so close!

"We just passed the final marker. End of the runway!" Vogel called out.

"Just a little longer," he replied, intentionally filling his voice with an optimism he no longer felt.

Gutwein held the nose down a bare moment more. Ahead of them, the final warning lights that marked the end of the runway flashed. Tense and anxious before — now, his smile was genuine. He had done all he could. Fate would decide whether his aircraft could fly.

Vogel stared at him, terror in his eyes. "End of the runway!"

Gutwein's smile turned into a broad, lunatic grin. He pulled the yoke ever so gently toward his chest. The nose lifted slightly off the ground and he felt the massive change in force as the aircraft altered its angle. He carefully maintained some forward pressure to stop the nose from over extending and causing them to stall.

Pine trees lined the edge of the field, approximately five hundred feet past the end of the runway. By the time the Condor reached them, its landing gear were less than ten feet off the highest tree.

"Gear up," he ordered.

"Landing gear raised," Vogel acknowledged, as he moved the lever.

The mechanical actuators whined loudly as the taildragger's wheels folded backwards into their nacelles under the inboard engines.

In the rear-facing engineer's seat, Krause glanced through the small viewing point in the flooring that gave him a clear view of the Condor's underbelly. "Gear up, and locked," he confirmed.

With the drag of the landing gear removed, the Condor was finally able to pick up speed and gain altitude. Gutwein set a course for a steady climb until they reached a cruising height of nine and a half thousand feet. Its technical ceiling was above twenty thousand, but without a pressurized cabin, they were restrained by the thin atmosphere to ten thousand feet.

Gutwein immediately set a northerly course and continued until they reached the English Channel. Vogel unclipped his harness. Taking the secondary role of radio-operator, he headed aft and waited for the report from Germany's radio tower at Bordeaux. The operator there had been instructed to broadcast any sightings of enemy aircraft throughout the entire region.

A few minutes later, Vogel returned and took his seat again.

Gutwein glanced at him. "Well?"

"We have a clear run down the Channel and into the Atlantic."

Gutwein closed his eyes and gave a silent prayer of gratitude. "That's a miracle."

He took the first shift for a total of four hours, flying over the Channel closer to the French Coast. With the blackout, there was little to see. No one would risk turning their lights on after dark since the war had begun and air raids were common. He passed the most eastern French peninsula of Brest and headed out into the dark Atlantic, setting the course they would try to maintain for the next twenty or more hours.

He unclipped his seatbelt. "Here, take the controls. Maintain this heading. I'm going to take my first sleep shift."

Vogel confirmed, "I have the controls. Have a good sleep, sir."

"Wake me if we run into trouble."

Gutwein headed to a somewhat flat section of floor toward the aft of the fuselage, where an inflatable mattress formed a poor replacement for a bed. For two hours he lay there with his eyes shut, trying to force himself to sleep. It was an impossible task. Within another twenty-four hours he might fail in his mission and that would mean he'd be dead. Alternatively, and somewhat more terrifying still, he might succeed, and perhaps millions would have died because of him.

Both outcomes were abhorrent. His entire mission abominable, but necessary. *"Wer die Wahl hat, hat die Qual,"* the German proverb advised, meaning, "He who has choice has torment."

Fortunately, he wasn't burdened by decisions. His choices had dwindled. They were narrowing further with every minute of flight.

After four hours and having checked his wristwatch for what

seemed to be the millionth time, he gave up. Gutwein stretched his legs, poured himself a coffee, and headed toward the cockpit.

He stopped midway along the shallow fuselage, where Krause was at the top of a small ladder taking a sighting through the observation dome above. Gutwein waited until Krause had finished and climbed back down.

"How are we looking?" he asked.

"Good," Krause answered. "Do you want to take your own sighting and confirm our coordinates?"

"Sure." He put his coffee mug down.

Gutwein took the bubble octant, which was basically a sextant, designed to work through the observation dome, and climbed up to the top of the ladder. The observation dome protruded a single foot above the top of the metal body of the fuselage. The sky was clear above and he had an uninterrupted view of the stars. It was another good omen.

He spotted Polaris and then adjusted the bubble until the octant appeared level. Making a note of the time, he looked through the mirror, adjusting the angle until the star appeared to be on the azimuth. He then read the angle off the mirror. Gutwein made a mental note of the angle and the time using a navigator's accurate chronometer. This number would later be used to calculate their longitude. He then spotted Sirius and followed the same process until he could accurately read off its angle. This number would be used to calculate their latitude.

Gutwein climbed down the ladder and sat down at the navigator's table. Krause handed him the book of navigation almanacs. He quietly flicked through the pages until he came up with the matching angles. Navigators measured distance on the globe in degrees, arcminutes, and arcseconds. A nautical mile is defined as 1852 meters, which is exactly one minute of angle along the meridian of the Earth.

He wrote the numbers down.

46°51'05.7" North

And,

21°42'51.9" West

He marked the coordinates on a map of the Atlantic and smiled. Krause had calculated the same numbers. The tail wind was making a considerable improvement in their ground speed. They were making good time.

Gutwein returned to the cockpit and took over the controls, sending Vogel off to try and get some sleep. The next four hours passed relatively quickly. The tail wind even picked up a little. So long as their luck held, they would make it with fuel to spare.

That's when Krause approached. His jaw was set hard, his concern was palpable.

"What is it?" Gutwein asked.

Krause swallowed. "We have a problem."

The Lorenz FuG 200 Hohentwiel low UHF-band ASV radar was a new addition to the Condor. Positioned in the nose of the aircraft, the device utilized an array of sixteen horizontally-oriented antennas, which the radio operator had to manually switch between to determine the direction of the enemy. The received signal strength was then displayed on a cathode ray tube, also called a monitor, so the observer or pilot could roughly gauge the target's heading. When it worked, it provided results bordering on the realms of what was considered magic, before the start of the war.

Gutwein felt the fear rise in his throat like acid after a long night drinking heavy whiskey, as he stared at the image.

"Is there any chance this is a false reading?" he asked.

"No," Krause said, without hesitation. "The exact location may be off slightly, but there's no doubt about it... we're on a direct heading for an enemy convoy."

Gutwein shook his head. Two years ago, this would have been exactly what they were looking for. Now there was too much risk that they would be shot down and the most important mission in the history of the war would be ignobly lost to bad luck.

Since 1941 Winston Churchill, who despised the Focke-Wulf 200 Condor as the *Scourge of the Atlantic,* ordered every convoy to carry an escort of Hawker Hurricanes. The small fighter planes were equipped with new Rolls Royce Merlin engines, and launched via the ship's CAM catapult system. Stripped of her defensive armor and weaponry, the Condor would be annihilated by their twin 40mm Vickers machineguns. Gutwein sighed heavily. "All right. We'll head north to avoid it. We're using less fuel than expected, we can afford a minor detour, yes?"

Krause shook his head. "Not possible. The predominant wind farther north is westerly. With a head wind, we'd never reach our target."

"Okay, so we go south."

"That's possible, but we'd have to go a long way south to avoid the trailing end of the convoy."

"We can do that."

Gutwein returned to the cockpit with the new bearings and advised Vogel to adjust his flightpath due south immediately. He wasn't taking any chances of the group of ships spotting them and making a precautionary attack. Right now, their only saving grace was the fact that by the sheer size of the convoy they had been able to spot them on radar at a distance of eighty miles, much too far for the convoy's radar to spot their small aircraft.

The Condor banked left and maintained that course for forty-five minutes before turning due west again. Gutwein joined Krause in the radio operator's station, and studied the cathode ray tube for any signs of the convoy changing their direction.

As he snuck around the enemy, he subconsciously found himself holding his breath, like a child might during a game of hide and seek. When they passed, his lips curled in an upward smile of success. If Winston Churchill had any idea what just slipped by him, he would have happily sacrificed his entire convoy just to stop their mission.

Half an hour later, Gutwein took over the controls again, as they set a new course toward their target. The rest of the flight continued uneventfully until they were about three hours from the coast of America — when thick cloud cover swept over them.

Gutwein tried to rise above the clouds, but they continued above their maximum unpressurized ceiling height of ten thousand feet. He dropped down to a cruising altitude of eight thousand feet and kept the yoke fixed steady, concentrating on keeping the Condor in a straight and level flying position. His eyes continuously scanned the artificial horizon, altimeter, and compass, to avoid deviating from their current readings on the instruments.

Pilots, disoriented by the sudden loss of any visual references, were prone to making fatal mistakes within minutes of entering dense cloud cover. Gutwein had been a pilot long enough not to lose his composure during such an event. The cloud would soon pass, at least by the time they reached the American coastline.

Once there, they could drop to a thousand feet and pick up their bearings from known topographical markers and reference points.

His eyes darted over the reserve fuel gauge. They still had time and fuel, but most of their calculations were based on making a direct route. With the clouds blocking Kraus's view of the stars, it would be impossible to take a sighting and calculate their position. Right now, he was using *dead reckoning* to navigate.

All he had to do was maintain the same heading and they would reach their target. The problem was aircraft, unlike a car, rarely maintained a specific course. Instead, the wind blew them one way or the other in a process called drifting.

Right now, Gutwein knew that the wind was approaching from north-east. He was certain that it was blowing him to the south and a little farther west, which was good. The problem was, how much was he drifting south? Ordinarily it wouldn't matter. If they had enough fuel reserves, they would continue on a bearing heading west until they reached the coast, and then follow the coastline to their target.

Their fuel supply was going to be close.

He looked at Vogel, who was trying to calculate their fuel on a pad of paper next to him. "Go wake Krause up for me. I need to get a more accurate idea of our rate of drift."

"Yes, sir."

Vogel returned with Krause a minute later.

Gutwein said, "The cloud cover's come in hard and we're trying to maintain our original heading. I need to know our rate of drift."

"Understood. I'll organize it for you now, sir."

Gutwein shook his head. "No. This is too important. I need to see it for myself. We all know what's riding on this. We need to be certain. I'll come with you." He handed the controls over to Vogel. "You have the controls. I'll be back in a few minutes. Take us lower until you have a visual on the sea and keep her there."

"Understood, sir."

Gutwein unclipped his seatbelt and followed Krause toward the tail stopping at the starboard wing. There, a hatch allowed them to climb inside the wing, crawling on their bellies — usually to provide maintenance on the engines while they were running. Midway along the wing, a trapdoor opened to the sea below.

Both men made their way to the trapdoor.

Krause held the unlit flare in his hand. "Are you ready, sir?"

"Yes. Go on."

Krause lit the flare and dropped it.

Gutwein watched as the burning flare fell into the water far below. If it had stayed roughly in line with the tail of the plane, it meant they were maintaining a steady course. As he expected, that wasn't the case.

The flare seemed to immediately move to the port side of the tail. The drift was strong. They would have to make a correction for it, but it would involve more guessing.

"Do you want me to drop another one, sir?"

Gutwein shook his head. "I've seen enough. We're being heavily blown to the south. We'll have to make a correction."

He made his way out of the wing and took over the control of the aircraft again. Gutwein increased their altitude to a more efficient cruising height of eight thousand feet. He chose a bearing slightly more to the north in an attempt to correct for the suspected drift. There was no clear science for how much to correct, though. Instead it was more a case of pilot experience and gut instinct. The problem was, instincts had the possibility of being wrong.

Three hours later, Krause knelt on the bulkhead just behind Gutwein's seat and handed him a notepad. "This is our current fuel reading."

Gutwein glanced at the notepad. The numbers were much worse than he'd predicted. *We can't be that low, surely?* He glanced back at Krause. "Are you certain?"

"I measured it twice." His voice was firm.

His eyes glanced at Vogel and back to Krause. A proud smile formed on his thinned lips and his eyes narrowed with defiance. "All right. Moment of truth gentlemen. We've either played our cards just right and we're now already over the coastline of America and close to our target — or we've failed our mission and our country."

He lowered the Condor's nose and made their descent. The cloud cover was still thick. He prayed that it would thin as they dropped their altitude.

They were in a complete whiteout.

Seven minutes later, and at a height of three thousand feet, the ground finally came into view. It was covered in thick snow and surrounded by jutting stones that formed the peak of a small mountain range.

His eyes narrowed. "Where are we, gentlemen?"

Krause opened the topographical map. His eyes swept the region of their target. It was impossible to see any identifiable navigation aids or markers. No signs of civilization, much less a city.

Gutwein brought them into a wide circular flight path, but the terrain below all seemed to place them in the middle of a low-level mountain range. On all the maps he'd studied, there weren't any mountains near their target.

He looked at his two men. His voice was full of accusation, but it was for himself and not his men. "Well? Where are we?"

Krause spoke first. "I've no idea, sir."

"Vogel?"

"No idea."

"All right. Look to the south of our target. We were drifting in that direction, so that's where we must be." Gutwein sighed and forced himself to smile. It felt fake, but there was nothing else that could be done. "I'm going to head north. We might yet find our target. Let me know when one of you work out where we are. No complaints. This was no one's fault. Let's just fix it."

"Yes, sir," they both replied.

The snow clouds thickened and Gutwein found himself flying straight into the mouth of a full-blown blizzard. His visibility reduced to near zero. His instruments beeped, warning of a buildup of ice. This was a heavy additional weight, as well as a deadly, fuel-consuming problem. Through the falling snow, the sea of white, undulating ground below, seemed to disappear.

He lowered the nose and took the Condor to a thousand feet. It didn't leave much room if they ran into trouble. Not that it mattered anymore, there weren't any other solutions left. Gutwein simply had to work with what he had. The blizzard blew stronger, and he struggled to maintain control of his aircraft, let alone work out their position.

After fifteen frenzied minutes of searching the landscape for some point of reference, the inevitable happened.

The portside engine number two skipped a beat, coughed, and choked to a stop. Gutwein didn't need to ask what had caused the sudden loss of power to his otherwise reliable German engine. They were out of fuel, and within minutes all four engines would cut out and his Condor would plummet to the earth.

His eyes searched the vile and inhospitable landscape below. He swallowed hard. "Okay, gentlemen. I'm going to need to find somewhere to put us down."

Vogel searched the winter landscape. "I can't see anything."

Gutwein yelled over his shoulder to Krause. "Get back into the bomb bay and remove the arming plugs. The last thing we want is for the damned bomb to reach critical mass on impact!"

Krause unclipped his harness. "I'm on it!"

There was nothing more Gutwein could do. He would have to ditch. *But could he protect his deadly cargo?* He knew nothing about this bomb, really. Would it explode on impact? Even that would be better than it falling into enemy hands. If he did land, could he retrieve it? Even if he did retrieve it, what did he know about the foul weapon? It wasn't like he could get it to the target by any other means, could he?

Gutwein forced himself to forget about secondary concerns. Right now, his job was to land the aircraft. If he could do that, he might just live long enough to overcome the other obstacles.

Engines number four, two and one sputtered to a stop, nearly simultaneously. He extended the flaps in an effort to reduce their touchdown speed. In doing so, it reduced their glide ratio. It didn't matter, they'd be hitting ground well before they could reach a suitable location to land.

"Anyone see anywhere to put us down?" Gutwein asked, his

voice almost conversational in his acceptance of his fate, as he scanned the undulating sea of snow and filtered caps of fir trees.

"I've got nothing," Vogel said.

"Pick a line through those trees. Any one of them. There's nothing we can do." There was no terror or fear in Kraus's voice. He was merely stating the truth. Even if they survived the crash, the surrounding landscape would kill them long before they could ever escape the region.

Vogel pointed to the south and asked, "What about that valley?"

Gutwein's head snapped to his right. His eyes swept the landscape where Vogel had pointed. Two shallow mountain peaks narrowed into a valley below. The slope was surprisingly gentle, and at the end of it, the area rose into a large saddle full of snow. If fortune favored them, they could land on it, their lethal momentum slowed by thick snow.

It was a lousy option, but it was the only one he'd seen since they'd come out of the cloud and spotted their mistake. Even the best gambler would eventually be left with only one option to play. This was his.

"All right. I'll take it." Gutwein smiled at both of his men. It was genuine and warm. "Your country may never know how much you sacrificed for her, but I do. It has been a privilege to fly with you over the past three years."

"Thank you, sir."

He banked to the left and set up for a final approach.

The Condor fell hard on a downdraft—for a moment he wasn't even sure he was going to clear the first peak. He didn't lower the landing gear, hoping that a smooth underbelly might slide along the snow-covered ground, like a ski.

Gutwein spoke gently. "Good luck and God bless."

The tip of the taildragger narrowly avoided clipping the peak of the mountain by less than a foot. Gutwein pushed the yoke forward and dipped the nose. The condor dropped downward into the shallow valley below.

Just before the belly of his craft touched the soft snow, Gutwein pulled the yoke backward. The Condor reluctantly flared, then sank into the deep snow, lurching as it landed. Momentum kept the Condor sliding forward, almost as fast as their final approach.

Holding his breath, Gutwein held on through the flurry of movement, waiting for his final greeting with death.

Two thirds of the way down the mountain, the thick snow appeared to finally be having some effect on their inertia, and the aircraft began to noticeably slow.

An instant later, the starboard wing clipped a large stone, buried beneath the snow — ripping it off, rotating the cockpit and fuselage forward in a sideways direction. Gutwein's harness dug tight into his waist as the cockpit spun round in an instant. The Condor struck a second boulder, ripping off the port wing.

Gutwein felt his head snap to the side, and his world became little more than a blur.

A second later, the cockpit and the Condor, no longer following the middle of the valley, ricocheted across the gorge, before plummeting into the side of the snow-covered mountain.

Everything went dark, as the Condor came to rest, apparently buried deep under thick snow.

Gutwein opened his eyes. A small trickle of blood ran across his forehead where he'd knocked it. He turned his head and brushed the blood off with his right forearm. He gently manipulated his hands and wiggled his toes. His head spun, but everything still worked.

I'm still here.

Was it chance when knowledge, experience, and preparation ran head-long into opportunity? Gutwein had lost his wife and children, drawn a suicide mission, been forced to take off during an air-raid, escaped a convoy's detection, run out of fuel, landed in the middle of nowhere, and ended with a couple of cuts and bruises, nothing more. With luck, they could complete their mission.

"Are you gentlemen all right?" he asked.

"I'm good," Vogel said. "Any idea where we put down?"

"What about you, Krause?"

"I'm injured, but I'll live. Any idea where we put down?"

Gutwein shook his head. "None whatsoever."

Vogel unclipped his harness and stood up. "And we won't know for some time. At least until this blizzard blows over. We'll need to take shelter in the Condor, prepare our survival equipment, and then see if we can trek out of here."

The lines around Gutwein's eyes wrinkled with a smile as he studied their snow-covered surroundings. "But at least we're on the ground."

A moment later, his smile disappeared.

The ground beneath them rumbled. Gutwein's gaze followed a giant rift in the ice, as it began to crack and ripple as if in an earthquake. Instinctively, he gripped the steering yoke and pulled up, as though he could avoid the giant opening in the ground below.

Gutwein, normally a calm man in any emergency, began to scream.

As did Vogel and Krause.

Their screams were drowned out by the ripping sound of their craft breaking up. The ground opened up in front of them. The nose of the Condor dipped forward—an enormous, vicious maw, preparing to swallow the Condor whole.

The majestic airliner once more started to move. It was slow at first—more like a skier tipping over the crest of a mountain— but it picked up speed quickly. Within the darkened nightmare, the Condor raced deeper into the bowels of the earth. Her occupants were thrown about like ragdolls as she slid ever deeper, colliding upon unseen walls like a toboggan in the night, until she finally came to rest in pitch darkness.

Gutwein opened his eyes, but there was nothing for him to see.

He inhaled slowly, held his breath for a moment, and exhaled. His ribs were sore, but he could breath. He grinned. There were tears in his eyes and he started laughing like a blubbering idiot. The insane guffaw of a madman narrowly defeating Death. Their mission had been a failure and they'd crashed into a mountain, but they'd somehow survived. He felt for the small flashlight in his right leg pocket of his flight suit and pulled it out.

He switched the light on and turned to face Vogel and Krause. "What a ride, hey?"

There was no response.

He stopped laughing and shined the flashlight at Vogel's face. His copilot's face appeared unharmed. There were no cuts or grazes. His eyes were wide open, as far as Gutwein could tell. Otherwise, the man might have been sleeping, except his face that was once full of life and expression, was now inanimate. His eyes stared vacantly into Death.

Gutwein unclipped his harness, climbing over broken detritus to go to him. His chest was still. Gutwein placed his hand on Vogel's neck. He could still feel the cold sweat on his copilot's skin. That was all he could feel. No matter how much he tried to find it, he couldn't feel a pulse.

Carefully stepping out from what had once been the cockpit, he shined his flashlight across the rear-facing engineer's seat. This time he didn't need to check for life. The seat was positioned at the edge of the starboard wing's bulkhead. When the Condor collided with a large buried stone, the fuselage had been pushed inside, directly where Krause had been sitting. The seat, along with what remained of his navigator's body, had become intermingled in one horrific tangle of human flesh and warped metal.

Gutwein felt his world begin to spin. He took a couple steps backward toward the narrow end of the taildragger and vomited.

There wasn't much in it. Other than black coffee and a bar of Swiss chocolate, he hadn't eaten since leaving Stuttgart. He tried to open the hatch, but it wouldn't budge. Shining his flashlight around the inside of the fuselage, he searched for a way out.

Panic slid through him, cold fingers of dread ran up his spine. He had to get away from possible suffocation, death, and his fear of being buried alive. He couldn't look at his men, they were too horrific to confront. *Why had his almighty chosen to keep him alive, while his men were killed?*

He finally wrenched open the tail trapdoor and climbed into the narrow alcove where the tail wheel could be manually released if the hydraulics failed. Gutwein dragged himself to the end, where a small maintenance hatch led to the outside world.

Gutwein fought with the latch. It was stuck, of course. He adjusted his position so that he could kick it hard. All his extreme built-up anger, passion and violence—from the loss of his family through to the more immediate loss of the men under his command. All of it came out on this one broken latch.

On his third vicious kick, the trapdoor broke free into an open void below.

Gutwein turned around again and shined his flashlight into the opening. The space appeared clear for a few feet, then it was covered in snow. He slid down into the ice-hardened snow. The space between the frozen ceiling and the snow-covered ground was a corridor a little higher than the top of the fuselage.

He crawled along it until he passed the end of the Condor's tail.

Once there, it opened up to a more comfortable height of the fuselage. He cupped his flashlight with his hand, and his world became enveloped in complete darkness again.

Where the hell am I?

Gutwein uncapped the flashlight and began following the direction in which the Condor had obviously entered some sort of tunnel. He looked at the ground. The Condor had dug its way across the frozen surface. There was something metallic beneath his feet.

He kicked at it with his boots. The ice covering the metal came free and he stopped to examine it. There were two rusted pieces of iron, running parallel to each other. *An old railway track?* Very narrow. This was never made for a train line.

Ah. Tracks for a minecart.

Of all the places to crash, the Condor must have slid directly into an old mine shaft. With the exception of the small amounts of snow dragged in by the Condor, the tunnel was dry, and noticeably warmer than the subfreezing environment outside. Gutwein shined his flashlight upward, along the tunnel, following the trail of ice and rockfall where the Condor's fuselage had ripped through the tunnel. He pulled the hood of his flight jacket tight and started to head for the surface.

It took more than an hour's walk to reach the entrance.

A wall of soft snow reached the ceiling of the tunnel. A series of splintered pine boards, the remnants of an old wall of rough sawn softwood, two by fours, littered the entrance, where the Condor had crashed through.

His eyes rolled across the carnage, settling on the remains of a single board with words written in red upon one side.

Gutwein picked up the old placard, wiped off the snow. The notice read:

MARYLAND MINE COMPANY—CLOSED.
NOT SAFE TO ENTER.
TRESPASSERS WILL BE PROSECUTED.

He recalled several private and government owned gold mines in Germany had been closed at the start of the war, because of fears it would distract the number of abled bodied young men from their war efforts.

Had the same thinking occurred in the United States?

If that was the case, and the mine had indeed been closed, there might just be a chance that the Condor wouldn't be spotted for some time. It could possibly be off limits until the next summer had passed, by which time, he could have removed the nuclear components of the bomb. He could still ready it for delivery to its intended target.

Gutwein's mind raced to the wings that had been stripped upon landing. They would be out there in the valley somewhere. He would need to take them apart and bury them within the mine shaft. After that, he would need to board up the entrance once more. If he could do all that, perhaps there was still a chance he could complete his mission.

Gutwein placed his gloved hands into the wall of snow and pulled. A small heap of snow fell on him. As expected, the recently broken snow was soft. He tried again, and more fell. There was still no sign of light, which meant he'd been buried deeply. How deeply, only time would tell. There was no reason to believe the crash hadn't caused an avalanche that had now covered the outside of the tunnel.

Either way, he wouldn't be able to dig through it with bare hands.

Gutwein returned to the Condor. Inside he searched the cargo hold for maintenance and survival equipment. He withdrew tool after tool, throwing each one aside as their apparent use failed to help him escape. At the bottom of the small hold were a few maintenance tools, including a hammer, which he might use to dig his way out through the ice.

It took another four hours to work his way through the wall of ice and snow and climb out into the open.

Outside, the sun was already setting.

There was nowhere for him to go today. He climbed back into

the tunnel and returned to his aircraft. There he retrieved two large carry bags. They were designed to help keep them all alive if they had achieved their mission.

It seemed like a waste at the time, but now he became curious. What had those in the SS Intelligence department thought to provide him that might just save his life?

He unzipped the first bag.

There was enough food for three persons to survive a month. Rationing it well, by himself he could survive several months — well into the spring, and even summer. He exhaled slowly and smiled. It removed the immediate rush to free himself from the confines of the mountain. There wasn't a lot of water, but he could always melt the snow. It would take time, but he could do it.

He ate a small meal of cold, dried food rations as he studied the topographical map. He used a pencil to circle the three potential low-lying mountains that were within their range. None of them was close to the target. It took a while, but by the time he was ready to go to sleep, he felt fairly confident he'd located the rough area of their crash site.

He was silently thankful for the difficult terrain. If it was hard for him to get out, it would be harder for someone to come in and locate his wrecked aircraft by accident. Perhaps he could still develop a plan to retrieve the bomb when the ice thawed in the summer? It might take a long time, but so long as he was still alive, there was still hope that he could complete the mission.

Gutwein opened the second backpack. He had already guessed what was inside. Now that he knew his immediate survival was no longer in jeopardy, the contents of the second bag would be more important to him.

There were three passports.

He selected the one that he was supposed to take. The name was William Goodson. He studied the American passport German Intelligence had provided him.

Would it still work?

So long as he didn't try to cross any borders, would anyone care to check?

If they did, would he be shot as a spy?

His eyes then turned to the counterfeit money. It was in the local currency. Abwehr, the German military intelligence service, had provided it. They had stockpiled a number of fake currencies throughout the war for spies. Of course, Gutwein's mission was the last to have any real consequence, so they'd simply stuffed a duffle bag with the American hundred-dollar notes. There was enough money there to allow him to live as a very rich man. So long as no one found the Condor, no one would ever believe that a German had flown across the Atlantic to start a new life.

He examined the first bundle. *Would they suffice, or would they, too, be discovered as fakes and seal his fate as a German spy ending in his execution?*

He shook these thoughts from his mind. They weren't his responsibility. Someone else had made the decisions which would ultimately determine whether he lived or died. He would need the identification papers and the money if he were to survive. His German officers in intelligence had either done their part well or not.

He loaded a backpack with survival rations, cash, and what had become his most treasured possession — a small, leather bound journal, in which he had documented the entire event.

He glanced at the strange bomb sitting in its purpose-built cradle. Studying it, he carefully ran his hands along the edge of it. The entire device appeared sound and intact. It had fared far better than the Condor or his men.

The big question remained, would it still work?

It would take time, but so long as he lived, he might still have a chance to complete his mission. It would just take a lot longer than he'd originally hoped.

His family, his friends, and his country had all been taken from him. He felt a terrible stab of shame, as he realized that he was thankful that his life had been spared. But perhaps he needn't feel guilty. Perhaps this was meant to be.

Luck. Fortune. Fate. Was there a reason he had been spared?

Gutwein's lips curled into a Machiavellian smile of purpose. God had given him the means and opportunity to finish his mission. Now, he had all the time in the world to take revenge on those who had taken everything from him.

CHAPTER ONE

GREEN-WOOD CEMETERY, NEW YORK—PRESENT DAY

Alex Goodson had always known he was different.

He had been an awkward kid. As a young adult, he fell short of being attractive, and a long way off being liked by anyone. He had blond hair, which he carefully combed with the precision that bordered on the wrong side of obsessive compulsion. He had a moderately pleasing face, with light blue eyes, a prominent nose and a strong jawline. His teeth were white and evenly spaced. His face bore the remnants of an acne-filled teenage-hood with a series of small pockmarks. The rest of his skin was an unnatural and sickly pale color—the result of inadequate exposure to sunlight rather than disease.

He spent most of his time in front of computers, where he didn't have to interact with other people. Despite his apparent lifestyle of inactivity, he had the sort of wiry physique that never really filled out to match his clothes. As a consequence, his suit today appeared conspicuously big for him.

The weather was pleasantly warm for early spring, approaching 75 degrees Fahrenheit. Speckled sun filtered through the new foliage of the red oak trees that lined the southern pathway. The unique fragrance of blossoming magnolias filled the air. Alex couldn't quite place the smell. To him, it smelled like tropical fruit—something between mango and papaya.

Breathing in deeply through his nostrils, he grimaced as he stood waiting through the funeral service. The overly sweet fragrance seemed unnaturally strong this morning.

The priest droned on. The people in the crowd had their eyes down in prayer.

Alex didn't listen. Instead, his eyes rolled along the row of juniper trees that lined the south path as it meandered down the undulating hills of the cemetery. Somewhere in the vicinity of six hundred thousand graves filled those mounds. Alex smiled as he imagined the colorful lives of those who were buried. Some struggled to succeed in life, others were rich, some talented, others were merely unlucky—all were now dead.

Something about the concept amused his morbid curiosity. It brought home the simple concept that whatever we achieve on earth, we all end in nothing. His mind wandered aimlessly. He recalled that the hill was once the very spot where the Battle of Long Island was fought in August 27, 1776. The first major encounter of the American Revolutionary War to take place after the United States declared its independence on July 4, 1776. It was a victory for the British Army and the beginning of a successful campaign that gave them control of the strategically important city of New York. In terms of troop deployment and fighting, it was the largest battle of the entire war.

The background murmur stopped. The Catholic service had finished.

Alex closed his eyes for a moment and tried to remember what he was supposed to be doing. These things came easily to others, but this sort of thing was foreign to him—he had to put on his act and give the performance that was expected of him. He felt confident he could do it. It just took a little more effort than it did for everyone else, that was all.

The dull thud of soil falling on wood made him open his eyes. Alex watched as the first pile of soil was being shoveled onto the lowered casket. His face was impassive, unemotional, and unreadable.

Alex glanced at the faces of those who surrounded the pit. They were staring at him, but their expressions weren't impassive. He could read those expressions with ease. They looked at him as though he was a monster. They may as well be speaking out loud — they said, "How come this fucked up kid can't even cry at his own father's funeral?"

Alex smiled. It's what he'd learned to do when he felt awkward. He had a nice set of teeth — always diligent with the brushing, you know — and somehow his smile generally set people at ease.

He saw instantly it was a mistake. In this case, it seemed to do the opposite. People seemed to be even more confused by him. Whatever he was doing, it appeared wrong to those watching. Alex knew he was so different, he simply didn't know what sort of emotion he should be feeling, given the circumstance.

The truth was, he didn't know how he felt about his father's death. He'd never been close to the guy. He was never quite up to the old man's standard, whatever the hell that was supposed to be. His father had treated him kindly. It wasn't as though he'd been an angry man or violent toward him. It was more a case that his father had no idea what to do with him. When Alex recalled his father looking at him, it was as though the old man was filled with regret and disappointment. Deep down, Alex was grateful that his father had at least tried to hide those things from him.

Alex scanned those faces again that looked upon him now as people departed. Some awkwardly walked past him without saying a word. Others provided him with some sort of meaningless physical gesture. A pat on the shoulder, a gentle embrace of the arms, or an overtly dutiful handshake. Some of the people, he knew. Others, he could guess where they'd come from. Some men and women were in uniform, from the days when his father had flown helicopters in the Vietnam War.

Others had been friends of the family for years.

There was one man who Alex definitely didn't recognize. An older man, who wore an expensive suit and split his time evenly between checking his watch and glancing up at Alex, as though waiting for an invitation to speak. When the man finally accepted Alex wasn't going to invite him, the man approached on his own accord.

The man offered his hand. "I'm sorry for your loss, Mr. Goodson."

Alex took it and met the stranger's light gray eyes. There was no sign of sadness, like the other guests. Alex asked, "Were you responsible for my father's death?"

"No. Goodness no. Of course not!" The stranger was startled by the absurd question. "What are you talking about? I was told he had a heart attack in his sleep!"

Alex nodded in confirmation. He had no doubt foul play was involved. "Then you have nothing to feel sorry about. It wasn't your fault." Alex paused, unsure how to address the stranger. "Mr.–"

"Whipple. Abel Whipple."

Alex nodded. He'd never heard the name before, which meant he'd never met this man. Despite his often stumbling, artless behavior, Alex had an eidetic memory. "How did you know my father?"

"I'm afraid I didn't. Not really. I knew of him, but that's a very different thing than knowing a person, isn't it?"

Alex nodded again. Not really understanding what the man meant, he remained silent.

"I'm a lawyer, you see," Abel continued. "If it's not too much to ask, given all the trouble you must be going through, could I arrange a time for you to come by my office?"

"Why?"

"I'm sorry I wasn't more forthcoming when we first met. I'm not really here for your father. I'm here to see you."

"Me?" Alex smiled, making the curve of his lips appear genuine, but it was as practiced as any actor. "What do you want from me?"

"You are the beneficiary of a certain will. As executor, I'd hoped to attend this matter as soon as it is reasonably convenient for you."

The executor of my father's will. So that's why he's here.

"How about right now?" Alex asked.

Abel's bushy eyebrow's narrowed. "Now?"

"Sure. Why not?"

"Mr. Goodman, don't you want to attend the wake?"

"No." Alex's blond brows drew down as he stared at the distressed, sorrowful, and somewhat baffling faces of those who probably knew his father better than he ever did. "There's nothing left for me here."

Abel looked up at him, his smile obsequious. "Very good, sir. Now would be perfect."

Confused by this form of address, as well as being the recipient of an attitude and facial expressions he'd never experienced, Alex didn't understand what they meant. Only one thing seemed clear: the man must be a very expensive lawyer.

CHAPTER TWO

THE YELLOW CAB stopped out in front of a large building at the corner of Fifth Avenue and East Street in New York City. Alex followed the lawyer through the revolving doors, past the glistening lobby and into a private elevator with a waiting attendant. The lawyer, content that he'd achieved his goal in herding Alex to his own office, remained silent throughout the entire trip. It would have made most people uncomfortable, but Alex found the lawyer's reticence comforting.

He rode the elevator to the top floor, where the lawyer stepped out. The entire office appeared more like a luxurious penthouse than a law firm. It had floor to ceiling glass in every direction, giving expansive views of Central Park. A large placard in golden writing identified the firm as *Whipple and Easley*. Alex noted the name of the Prestigious law firm and wondered what the hell his father could possibly have to do with such a place. A woman in her mid-forties approached. She was impeccably dressed in a tailored suit and spoke with the refined authority of someone who'd studied at an Ivy League university.

She smiled politely and glanced at him with immediate recognition. "Good afternoon, Mr. Goodson. I'm sorry for your loss. My name's Rebecca Thompson. I'll be joining Mr. Whipple to execute the last will and testament of the late Mr. Goodson."

Alex met her professional cordiality with his practiced smile.

"Good afternoon."

"May I organize a drink, or refreshments to be brought up for you?" she asked.

"No, thank you." Alex dropped into a chair in a boardroom styled office, at the edge of a table that offered at least twenty seats. Opposite him, the two lawyers took their seats. He glanced around the room. Everything about it said mega-expensive—from the rich mahogany table, down to the lavish carpet and gun barrel view of Central Park.

"I'm sure you both have more pressing matters. I'm here to see what request my late father has made of me that he couldn't ask me in person, and then I'll be off."

Whipple smiled. It was surprisingly warm. His previous unctuous façade pulled back, leaving an expression of real disbelief. "Mr. Goodson, why do you think I asked you to come here today?"

"To execute the last will and testament of my late father. Although, to be honest, how he managed to afford your services honestly dumbfounds me."

"I'm sorry, son, were you under the expectation you are here at the bequest of your late father?"

"Yes," Alex said, studying their faces, unable to read their expressions.

Abel Whipple took a deep breath in and exhaled slowly. He spoke with an unreserved sympathy. "Your grandfather, Mr. William Goodson was in fact our client. I'm afraid I never had the privilege of meeting your father when he was alive."

At the mention of his grandfather, Alex felt his heart speed up. "My grandfather died nearly ten years ago. Why are you contacting me now?"

"Mr. William Goodson retained our services throughout the past forty years of his life. But it was only the year before he died that he took on a very specific request for our assistance." Whipple made a big show of taking a deep breath and sighing.

"You see, he wanted you to receive some items of particular importance to him."

Alex felt incredulous. In his logical world, this made no sense. "Why now and not ten years ago?"

Whipple shrugged as though it wasn't his place to wonder at such things. "Your grandfather was quite explicit. You weren't to receive the items in question until after your own father should pass — of course I'm certain he didn't expect his death to occur so soon."

Alex had known his grandfather well. In many ways, he knew the older man much better than he had his father. Where his own father was impatient with his inability to achieve normality in society, his grandfather simply accepted him as he was. "Do you know what he left?"

"I'm afraid not. Your grandfather was explicit that the contents of this safe-deposit box should never, under any circumstances, ever be discovered by your father — and certainly not by me." The lawyer lowered his head and winked. "You know how it can be."

Alex gave him a practiced and reassuring nod, although he had no idea what the damned lawyer meant. "Sure. All right. What do you need me to sign?"

The two lawyers handed him several papers and he happily signed each one without reading it at all. His grandfather had entrusted this man with something he felt very strongly about, and the man had maintained this secret for nearly three decades. He was happy to trust him, even if he was a lawyer.

Whipple and Thompson signed next to his signature, checked that everything was in order. Then they both pushed to their feet and left. Only Whipple returned, carrying a single manila envelope. He handed it to Alex. "I hope you find whatever it was Mr. Goodson wanted you to find in there."

"Sure," Alex said. "I can't imagine what that should be." He tore the envelope open and found a single piece of paper with a set of numbers followed by a brass key. He looked up at the lawyer. "What's this about?"

Whipple smiled patronizingly. "I'm sorry, you didn't think I actually stored it with us all those years, did you?"

"If it's not here, then where is it?"

"In a safe-deposit box, Wells Fargo Bank, 363 Broadway."

CHAPTER THREE

ALEX CAUGHT THE subway to Lower Manhattan. He then walked the three blocks to the address Whipple had given him. His face was set hard and impassive, hiding his inner turmoil. He had been quiet and reserved ever since the meeting with the lawyer. It didn't make any sense whatsoever. His grandfather had been dead for nearly a decade and his father less than a week. Why should he be so worked up over his grandfather?

He knew the answer of course—his grandfather had made the time to see him and had been opposed to sending him to military boarding school at the age of five.

He stopped and glanced up at the large red and yellow Wells Fargo sign above the entrance. Brass surrounded glass walls and doors, revealing a mixture of old school and modern banking. Alex stepped inside.

Clean. Opulent. Legitimate. If there was such a thing as the smell of money—this place had it. A glance around the room, and he felt out of place.

Alex waited in a short queue to see a teller.

When his turn arrived, he stepped up and greeted the teller and gave her his safe-deposit box number. She asked him to take a seat on one of the leather couches provided, and that someone would meet him shortly to discuss the matter.

Alex thanked her and took a seat.

Five minutes later, the manager — a short and portly man with a moustache that reminded him of the banker from the board game, Monopoly — ran his eyes across Alex. There was a slight amount of recognition in the man's face, followed by a broad smile.

Alex stood up. "I think you're after me."

"Mr. Goodson!" the bank manager embraced his hand warmly, like an old friend. "My name is Peter Doran. I was so very sorry to hear about the loss of your late father."

"You knew my father?" Alex asked.

"No. I'm afraid I didn't. But I had a close working relationship with your grandfather. He was quite explicit how he wanted to leave something for you and that it had to be after your father died. I wasn't quite certain I would ever get to meet you, I'm retiring next week."

"Congratulations." Alex made a show of his white teeth as his lips formed the smile he thought the response required. "What are you going to do with your retirement?" he asked, as he had learned was the correct thing to do.

"I'd like to make time to do some of the things I should have done in the last forty years of my life. Read the books I like, make the time to spend with my grandchildren that I didn't get to spend with my own kids, maybe even take my wife on a European vacation." The bank manager met Alex's eye with a polite smile. "Do you have kids?"

"No."

"When you do, let me offer you some advice — make the time to be with them. You'll never regret it, no matter how important you feel your work is."

"Okay, I'll do that," Alex replied, with a practiced curve of his lips. "When I have children."

There's no way I'm ever having children, dirty, nasty little creatures that they are...

"I'm sorry, I digress," the bank manager apologized. "Now. You must be curious what this is all about?"

He smiled patiently. "Yes. To be honest today was the first I'd ever heard about it."

"Of course, of course, you're right." The banker opened the doors of a private elevator for him. "If it makes you feel any better, it pleases me to hear that. You see, that means your grandfather's wishes were followed exactly as instructed."

Alex walked behind the banker, stepping into an elevator. The banker explained the procedure while the lift descended what appeared to be several stories below ground. There, he would be left in the private depository on his own, where his key would grant him access to his grandfather's safe-deposit box. Each box worked on a digitally managed, rotating system. Only Alex's safe-deposit box would be accessible, despite the vault presumably storing hundreds of identical such boxes.

The banker held the doors and waited for him to step out of the elevator. "When you're finished here, Mr. Goodson, simply press the up-button. Then I'll return to show you the trust your grandfather left you."

"My grandfather left me a trust?" Alex was skeptical of such a gift.

"Yes." The old banker smiled. "And from what I understand, it's large enough that you're unlikely to spend it within your lifetime."

Alex fixed his eyes on the banker. "He left me a lot of money?"

"Much more than I ever earned in my forty-five years at the bank."

"My grandfather barely had a dime to his name, he died in a rented apartment in the Bronx. If there's money here, you must be giving it to the wrong guy."

"You are the correct recipient, Mr. Goodson, I can assure you. And concerning his wealth or lack of it, you're very much mistaken."

Alex gave up. Whatever his grandfather did or didn't leave him, he would discover within due time. Talking to the kindly old banker served him no further purpose.

He sighed heavily. "All right. I'd better take a look at what my grandfather has left for me."

The banker stepped into the elevator and nodded. "Of course, of course. Remember, just press this button when you have finished."

Alex watched the steel elevator doors close. The entire elevator was built into the vault, so that as it rose, the platform disappeared into the ceiling above, making it overtly apparent that no one from the bank could have remained to spy on him. But Alex was cynical enough to suspect that there would be slyly concealed cameras to monitor the bank's interests, anyway.

He stepped closer to the base of the elevator and looked up. The dark shaft rose high into the basement of the main building. When the elevator finally came to rest at least twenty stories above, a large metallic door slid across the ceiling, entombing him in the bank's vault.

Alex's lips curved into his first genuine smile for the day as he glanced around the wall to wall metallic room. The entire place appeared sterile as a surgical operating theatre. The room even smelled of disinfectant, like a hospital. It was as though the people who stored their most valuable possessions in this place, wanted to wipe away their fingerprints and DNA — erasing all evidence of their presence. Actually, not so far-fetched, his cynical side noted.

Taking his single brass key out of his pocket, Alex stared at it. The thing looked out of place in this modern bank building. It belonged to the lock of a pirate's treasure chest.

What were you involved in, grandfather?

Alex grinned for the second time today.

The people who banked here weren't only storing their most valuable possessions. They were storing secrets.

He spotted the façade of a single locked box — the only one visibly different in the entire vault. On it was an electronic keypad. Next to which, was a single keyhole.

Alex read the note below:

> INPUT SAFE-DEPOSIT BOX NUMBER AND INSERT KEY.
> ONE ATTEMPT ONLY. INCORRECT MATCH AND ITEM WILL BE LOCKED PERMANENTLY.

Alex confirmed the safe-deposit box number, inserted the brass key he'd received, and turned the key. Despite the outwardly old appearance of the key, the boxes were futuristic and advanced. The façade disappeared into the dark alcove behind the vault. Roughly thirty seconds later, the original safe-deposit box was replaced with a new façade.

This one was simply identified by the number Alex had input.

He put his hand on the small metallic handle and pulled. The safe-deposit box remained rigidly fixed. A moment later, the box glowed red and the entire room was scanned by some sort of laser. Alex glanced around the chamber as more than a thousand laser beams crisscrossed throughout the vault, as though it was confirming the number of persons inside the room and their location. Seemingly content with its findings, the computer then released the drawer which slid effortlessly outward.

What were your secrets, grandfather?

Alex looked inside the box.

A single leather-bound journal stood in the middle. He opened it. The first page had a handwritten message addressed to him.

> *Dear Alex,*
>
> *I'm sorry for the loss of your father. Despite your differences, he loved you very much. This journal explains everything. Please read it carefully. I am certain you will know what must be done and that you will achieve what I could not within my lifetime. Good luck.*
>
> *Your loving grandfather, Wilbert Gutwein.*

CHAPTER FOUR

THE PENTAGON, VIRGINIA

Sam Reilly had never been a big fan of the Washington D.C. area, but that didn't matter, because his father hated the place. Ever since Sam had joined the family business, his father made him run all the company's errands in D.C. For a guy obsessed with money and power, Sam's father was practically paranoid about going anywhere near the place.

Which wasn't to say that Sam knew the area all that well. He knew the strip of road from the Ronald Reagan Airport to the Pentagon and a few similar places very well indeed—but that was about it.

One of the Pentagon drivers had picked him up, barely speaking once he made sure he had the right passenger. Sam was used to it. Many people around here acted like saying "good morning" was the same as giving away state secrets.

Despite the heavy traffic, it wasn't long before he had reached his destination. Able to comfortably accommodate hundreds in its lobby, the building was immense. Sam was whisked through a security line, then escorted to the office of the Secretary of Defense, a large room with blue carpet, a massive desk, and two small tables for meetings—four seats each. It wasn't the kind of place for a big, open meeting. Just a few generals and maybe a head of state or two. Secrets passed through this unpretentious, innocuous room day and night.

The door was closed by an aide. They were alone. The inconspicuous air-tight seal made Sam's ears pop.

The Secretary of Defense greeted Sam with a firm handshake. She was a slim but muscular woman with stark red hair. Intelligent, commanding, and often intimidating, she wore her dark business suit and her permanent scowl with equal severity.

"Thanks for coming on such short notice, Sam." As soon as she released his hand, she added, "What do you know about the German nuclear weapon project during World War II?"

Sam blinked. "Not much, ma'am, except that in the early 1930's, a scientist named Werner Heisenberg was awarded a Nobel Prize for the creation of quantum mechanics. He paved the way for the atomic bomb. I understand that Germany had a nuclear weapons project, but they were unable to progress to a completed prototype."

She nodded. "Exactly. We were informed that they didn't have enough D20, or heavy water. Heavy water has the same chemical formula as any other water, H20, except one or both of the hydrogen atoms are the deuterium isotope of hydrogen instead of the regular protium isotope."

Sam laughed. "I'm a little rusty on my chemistry, but if you say so, ma'am."

She ignored his comment. "Norsk Hydro built the first commercial heavy water plant at Vermork, Tinn, also in the early nineteen thirties. Since Norway was under German control during the war, Norsk Hydro were obliged to provide the German Nuclear Weapons Project its needed supply of heavy water."

"But the water went dry?"

"On February 27, 1943 the British led Operation Gunnerside succeeded in destroying the heavy water plant."

"And that's what saved the world from a nuclear Germany in World War II?"

The Secretary of Defense cocked an eyebrow. "You have no idea how close that statement is to the truth. Since the discovery of nuclear fission in late 1938, deuterium oxide—aka heavy water—has been used as a neutron moderator that captures neutrons."

Sam stared at her. "And that's useful for making an atomic bomb, because?"

The Secretary of Defense scowled. "Sit, sit. We may as well be comfortable."

Sam pulled out a chair for her. Once she was seated, he dropped down into the comfortable leather chair next to her.

"There are two ways to make a nuclear weapon. Through isotopic separation of U-235 from natural uranium, you can develop weapons grade uranium, which can then be used to make a nuclear bomb. Alternatively, and by far the fastest and cheapest route is to breed and extract plutonium." The Secretary of Defense frowned at Sam's puzzled expression and sighed. "Heavy water slows down neutrons. A fast neutron will not be captured by a uranium-235 nucleus. Thus, neutrons must be slowed down to increase their capture probability without fissioning."

"Which produces weapons-grade plutonium?"

"Exactly."

Sam poured ice water from a pitcher into a tumbler. He arched an eyebrow in question, but the Secretary just shook her head. "So without access to heavy water, the German nuclear weapons project was bound for failure."

She nodded. "Exactly. "The Uranium Club, as it was known, didn't really get going until 1939. At that time, they were turned over to the Reich Research Council in a reduced capacity in 1942 because they weren't producing enough results to satisfy the Führer."

"No results, huh?" Sam drank half the glass, placing the tumbler down on the fine deep brown table. Apparently, no one was worried about damaging the polish. "It turns out that when you send all your Jewish scientists to concentration camps, it slows down your research."

She gave him a stiff smile in acknowledgement. "In the spring of 1945, American troops raced through the area where the program had been moved. There, they captured or destroyed a lot of paperwork, equipment, and a prototype nuclear reactor—all which they brought back to Oak Ridge. By August, the Manhattan Project had developed the technology needed to make *Little Boy* with which we used to bomb Hiroshima, and *Fat Boy*, which we dropped on Nagasaki. Do you know anything about *Die Koloratursoubrette?*"

"No, ma'am, nothing whatsoever."

The secretary pushed to her feet and began to pace back and forth on that blue carpet, a floor that had been trod in worry many times over the years. She said, "On April 22, 1945, Colonel Boris Pash commanded the Alsos Mission—an Allied team of military, scientific, and intelligence personnel to determine enemy scientific developments during World War II and specifically, the progress of the German nuclear energy project—after rendezvousing with the 1269th Engineer Combat Battalion at Freudenstadt, crossed the intact bridge at Necker River in Horb, and set his eyes on the small German town of Haigerloch."

"I've heard of Haigerloch. Didn't they find the remains of an experimental nuclear reactor in an old barn there?"

"Hidden in the beer cellar of a castle in the small south German town of Haigerloch, to be exact," the Secretary of Defense corrected. "As you can guess, the team dismantled the machine and took it back to Oak Ridge, where the scientists from the Manhattan Project reverse engineered some of its specifications to overcome their own barriers."

Sam nodded. "I'm sure I read about it somewhere, years ago."

"What you probably didn't read about though, was that

when Colonel Boris Pash finally captured Werner Heisenberg at his retreat in Urfeld, on May 3, 1945, he discovered a set of plans for a fully functional nuclear weapon."

"Germany had engineered a functioning nuclear bomb?"

"Yes. They beat us to its development by nearly six months. If it wasn't for the luck of a fire in Haigerloch, which destroyed their heavy water reserves, Germany would have been able to produce multiple nuclear weapons. Just think what sort of outcome that would have meant for the Allies in World War II? We might be living in a very different world."

"A horrifying thought." Sam shook his head. "What's this all about, ma'am?"

The Secretary of Defense answered without hesitation, "There's a young man, named Alex Goodson."

"I don't know that name, either, ma'am."

Her lips formed a curt smile. "One day, he's nobody special — a computer geek who likes to play video games, a young man placed on the high-functioning end of the Autism spectrum. He's bright, antisocial, but not a big achiever."

"Go on."

"The next day, his father dies, and he's called to Manhattan — an inauspicious and rather ominous name in this case — as sole beneficiary of a will. Not his father's will, but his grandfather's. His grandfather was a German immigrant originally named Wilhelm Gutwein who changed his name to William Goodson when he arrived here during World War II, using forged papers."

Sam raised his eyebrow in incredulity. "Running from the Nazis?"

"No. Not at all. He arrived here in a plane, a Focke-Wulf 200S Condor."

"Wait a sec, I've heard of the Condor." Sam closed his eyes trying to remember what he'd read about the unique aircraft that seemed so familiar to him. "That's right, wasn't it a big plane used in trans-Atlantic travel before the war? The Germans converted them into bombers."

The secretary replied, "That's right, Sam. He was sent here by the Germans on January 12, 1945, on a mission to bomb Washington, D.C. His cargo was a unique weapon, one that had never been used before."

"You've got to be kidding me!" Sam swallowed. "Are you telling me the Germans had nuclear bombs before the end of World War II?"

"Bomb. Singular." The Secretary of Defense stopped pacing and gave Sam a level-eyed stare. "That's exactly what I'm saying, Sam. Alex Goodson has just discovered, via his grandfather's will, that his progenitor was a German pilot trying to attack the United States with an experimental nuclear bomb."

Sam shook his head. "I can't believe it."

"It gets worse."

"Go on."

"Our recent intelligence is that the bomb arrived in the country, but obviously, didn't explode."

Sam's skin went cold. "So, it's still sitting out there, somewhere?"

The secretary put her hand over her face for a moment and sighed. "A few days ago, Alex Goodson posted a topographic map online, which he'd found in his grandfather's journal. In the image the site of the wreck was identified with a small note stating a German bomber plane crashed here in 1945. Next to that, he posted a simple question, *anyone know where this place is?* Within a few hours, the first treasure hunters had started their search. By the next day there were hundreds, exploring the region for the lost aircraft."

"Do we have an operation on site?"

"Yes. There's a specialist team from the 832nd Ordnance Battalion US Marine Corps out of Fort Lee, Virginia, there now. All the treasure hunters and residents have been removed."

"Have they found anything?"

"A wrecked Condor, buried deep within the Maryland Gold Mine, located near the Great Falls of the Potomac."

"And," Sam paused, cleared his suddenly dry throat. "Did they find the bomb?"

"Not yet. They're still searching the wreck."

The phone started to ring on her desk. She strode over, picked it up. "What did you find?" The question came out as hard and fast as machine gun fire.

After a brief, one-way conversation, she said, "I understand," and hung up the phone.

Sam stood up. "What is it? Did they locate the bomb?"

"No. It had already been moved. The wreckage was located, including an empty bomb bay."

"So, the bomb was dropped — Lord knows where — it didn't go off, and has remained hidden in some old building, junk yard, or in someone's back yard?"

"No. Its cradle had been carefully dismantled manually and the bomb transported. We searched the crash site. No sign of radiation was discovered."

"What was it, then? Some other type of weapon?"

"I misspoke," the secretary said. "No signs of the bomb's physical components were found. Geiger-counter tests show that the bomb *had* been there at some point. It gave off radiation."

Sam shook his head again. "What are you telling me?"

"I'm telling you that someone beat us to the bomb, Sam." The Secretary of Defense sighed, heavily. "And now we have a *Broken Arrow* right here within the vicinity of Washington, D.C."

CHAPTER FIVE

A *Broken Arrow* was an unexpected event that involved nuclear weapons or nuclear components, resulting in the accidental launching, firing, detonating, theft, or loss. To date the U.S. Department of Defense has officially recognized thirty-two Broken Arrow incidents, with the revelation about this latest one making it thirty-three.

Sam felt bile rise in his throat.

On top of the seven-hundred-thousand permanent residents of the capital city, Congress was currently in session. There was little doubt in his mind about the intended target if a terrorist organization possessed a working nuclear weapon.

After the incredible adventures that Sam had survived in the last few years, he should have been able to handle the idea. However, like the rest of the world at the time, he had grown up under the fear of nuclear destruction. It was a fear that had literally haunted his childhood nightmares, he found that it chilled him even more than other threats he had faced.

Staring at the pitcher of water, Sam wondered if he should pour himself another drink.

"Would you like something stronger?" the Secretary of Defense asked, noticing the direction of his gaze.

He shook his head. "How long have you known?"

The secretary returned to her seat. "Less than three hours."

He poured himself another glass of water but didn't drink it.

Suddenly it seemed like he was riding a storm on a small boat being tossed in the waves. He put his tumbler down and stood up. It was his turn to pace the room.

His mind raced. "What have you done so far?" he asked.

"As soon as you arrived, we shut down the major roads, highways, tunnels, and airports. Everything inside the beltway, the metro, water traffic on the Potomac and Anacostia…"

He whistled. "Where, exactly, was the crash site?"

"Buried deep within an old disused gold mine, located at the Great Falls of the Potomac in Maryland."

"A gold mine?" Sam cocked an incredulous eyebrow. "How did it remain hidden for so long?"

"At the start of World War II, all gold mining activity was banned by the government nationwide as it was felt the manpower to operate a mine would be better used in the war effort. They originally planned to reopen the mine after the war, but this never happened."

"You're saying a failed German bombing attempt on Washington, D.C. resulted in a crash directly into one of these abandoned mine shafts?"

"Yes." The Secretary of Defense opened a map of the region dated late 1939. Sam came to her side, bent over to study the chart, his hand on the table.

"As you can see here," she said, "the whole area was riddled with open mine shafts. In January 1945 there was a massive eastern blizzard. The event resulted in a total whiteout. We believe that's the day the German FW Condor made its bombing run."

"If that's so, it makes sense," Sam said, "The pilot must have run out of fuel and put down in what appeared to be a gradually sloping field of white."

"Right," she acknowledged. "And then, unexpectedly the nose of the FW Condor fell through the boarded-up entrance to the mine shaft. Whereupon, the pilot escaped, and realizing what had happened, he hid the aircraft's wings—which were a metal and fabric composite—inside the mine, as well, to conceal his aborted mission and its cargo. He then re-boarded up the entrance, where the aircraft and nuclear bomb must've remained hidden ever since—well, until recently."

"Radiation, even at low levels, may have damaged the nearby plant life," Sam mused. "But it's been sealed off?"

"Completely."

"And how long are you going to be able to keep D.C. under lock and key?"

The secretary grimaced. "There's already an uproar, half an hour after you arrived. That's not your concern. We can deal with it."

The Washington D.C. area would be particularly susceptible to major problems from a lockdown of any sort—many of the people who worked in the area lived elsewhere. Including the members of Congress, which was currently in session. Sam didn't envy the secretary the job of trying to keep *that* group under control.

He set the thought aside. "What do you need me to do?"

He had half an idea of what she might need from him, but he suspected it would probably involve breaking a number of laws. If so, he needed her to be absolutely clear about what she needed.

She chewed on the inside of her cheek. "We have some very discreet, very intelligent people working on what possibly could have happened to the bomb and the various ways that such a thing could be brought past the Beltway without our knowing it."

"But you already know how it was done," Sam said.

"I have my suspicions."

"And?"

"How would you bring a nuclear weapon into the D.C. area, Sam?"

Sam's wry grin wasn't a happy one. "You *know* how I'd do it. I'd go straight along the Potomac River."

CHAPTER SIX

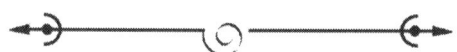

OFFICER JOHN DWYER was one of the four Virginia-based police officers who had been chosen to stand guard on the Chain Bridge over the Potomac. The cars had been parked at the intersection of North Glebe Road and Chain Bridge Road. The George Washington Memorial Parkway, which ran alongside the river and which passed over North Glebe Road, was packed nose-to-tail with traffic. North Glebe and Chain Bridge Road were busy, but nothing that the four of them couldn't handle — yet. If the situation went on much longer, it would cause nothing but problems.

A few minutes earlier, he had spotted movement in the green woods below the bridge. Several running and hiking paths ran through the trees nearby. Their orders had been to block off the Virginia end of the bridge, not to prevent anyone moving along the recreational trails, but he still thought he'd better take a closer look. Telling the others what he'd seen, he started moving back along the bridge, checking the rocky riverbank for a swimmer or a boat. Something small. Perhaps a canoe.

He didn't spot anyone, but he decided it wouldn't be a bad idea to have one of his men take a walk along the bridge to check every few minutes from now on.

He turned back to return to the others and froze.

One of the officers yelled back at him, "What is it? Do you see something?"

Officer Dwyer's mouth had fallen open. Surely, he must be going nuts or something...

"I'll be damned," he said.

"What is it?"

"A shark."

"Are you out of your ever-loving mind?" the other officer asked.

But there it was, a dark fin slicing through the surface of the water, heading downstream toward the bridge.

Officer Dwyer blinked as one of the other officers started to swear. He heard pounding footsteps running toward him.

No, not a shark—the top of a shark's fin wasn't squared off like that. Whatever was down there was man-made. Fortunately, it wasn't moving too quickly, and it was leaving a wake behind it that would be hard to miss.

He grabbed the shoulder of Officer Jackson, who had run up to stand next to him.

"Call that in, Jackson."

"Me? You're the one who spotted it. *You* try to explain it."

Officer Dwyer said, "The parkway's backed up all the way to the Francis Scott Key Bridge, Jackson."

"So?"

"So I'm going to follow the thing on the running trail. Unless *you* want to haul ass down there and run after it?"

Jackson, who was built like a Mac truck and huffed like he'd been running on the jogging track, shook his head. Officer Dwyer sent up a mental "thank you" to his father, who had always taken him jogging as a kid. Pleased to be generating some heat in the cool morning air, he ran to the end of the bridge, waved at the cars backed up on the overpass, and took off running along the trails.

A few minutes later his cell phone rang.

"Yes, ma'am," he confirmed to no less than the Secretary of Defense. "I still have the mini-sub in pursuit..."

CHAPTER SEVEN

THE SECRETARY OF Defense said, "Thank you, Officer Dwyer. Please keep it in sight at all times, if possible. We have sent out several drones as back up. You should be seeing them soon."

She paused.

"I'll take that into consideration. Thank you, ma'am."

She put down the handset. There was a fine tremor in her hand. *That's new.* She then let out an explosive breath.

"What is it?" Sam asked.

"One of the officers along the Chain Bridge called in with the report that another Officer had seen a shark in the Potomac."

Sam blinked. "A shark?" A flash of insight hit him. "A midget submarine! That's how they're moving the bomb into D.C.!"

"It seems that way," the secretary said, sounding unusually hesitant and uncertain. "We don't have time to put together a team or anything else to be able to prevent it from destroying the whole area. It's already in position, although if they moved just a little further south, they'll be able to do more damage."

"Get me on a helicopter!" Sam said excitedly, in a loud voice that was nearly a shout.

"Sam, it's too late. We need to concentrate on evacuation instead."

"Just get me out there. I've got an idea."

The secretary picked up the phone, then tossed it into a chair and stepped out of the office door. "Henriks! Get me a helicopter pilot out on the pad *now!*"

Sam knew his way and was already running full-speed down the halls.

CHAPTER EIGHT

IN MOMENTS, SAM was approaching the Pentagon's helicopter pad. A VH-60N Black Hawk converted to VIP use was waiting on the helipad, engine running, rotors slowly turning.

Sam spotted a single-link steel chain crossing the paths between the pad and the walkway leading up to it, and quickly unhooked it on both sides. About fifteen feet of chain in total. — *it might just be enough.*

People waiting to receive VIPs leaving the danger area via helicopter were just going to have to take their chances on getting too close to the machines. He had a plan for that chain. He wrapped it around his chest — cold, heavy links. The weight reassured him.

The Secretary of Defense caught up to him as he was heading for the Black Hawk.

"Sam Reilly, what are you going to do with that?" she shouted.

"You'll see."

Bent over, the two of them jogged up to the helicopter. Sam started to climb in.

An airman intercepted them, standing in Sam's way. "Stop! What are you doing?"

The secretary waved the pilot down. "We're appropriating this chopper! It's of national importance!"

The pilot was already shaking his head. "No can do, ma'am. Every one of the twenty-six helicopters of the 12th are en route to the Capitol to extract designated public servants as part of the Continuity of Government Plan. I'm pretty sure that this man's not on the list."

"You don't understand," the secretary started to say.

Sam interrupted the argument. "No problem, Captain. I just need a ride to the Potomac. You can drop me off on the way to Capitol Hill."

CHAPTER NINE

A FEW CURT words over the pilot's headset and they were on their way. It sounded like this pilot was engaged to assist in White House evacuation. Whatever vital function was being sacrificed or delayed to carry out Sam's plan, he didn't ask.

Within two minutes, they were above the Potomac, flying upstream.

"Any word on where the sub is now?" Sam asked the secretary through his headsets. The Black Hawk was fast, but noisy.

"The officer trailing it on foot lost sight of it near Bear Island in the Potomac Gorge. He states it submerged completely under the water at that point."

Sam shook his head. Something about the situation wasn't right. The two of them leaned over the sides of the helicopter, searching for evidence of movement.

She asked, "See anything?"

It was a bright and sunny day. Sam peered into the clear water to the brown riverbed. "Not yet."

They passed the Francis Scott Key Bridge. Already traffic was a nightmare.

"Sam!"

He quickly switched to the secretary's side and looked into the deeper blue water. The ripples sparkled back at him. A rill of lighter water within the river caught his eye. At the head of it, a dark shape.

There's the midget sub.

"Get me down as low as you can," he shouted over the headset, then ripped it off.

The pilot dipped the nose and took the Black Hawk into a hover just above the water. Sam unwrapped the heavy chain from around his chest, forming it into a circular link that he could still hold. It was as good a position as Sam was going to get — just ahead of the path of the submarine.

Sam slid open the door, fighting a stream of wind.

Holding onto a support handle, he studied the location of the midget sub one last time. Ten feet under water, it was not the kind of thing he wanted to dive straight onto.

The pilot shouted something.

Sam could just catch the secretary saying, "The only thing he can do. He's sacrificing himself to save the rest of us."

Sam grinned as he had a plan. No one was getting sacrificed today, especially himself! They were coming up to the Three Sisters, three rocky islands, west of the Key Bridge. Now was as good a time as any.

Taking a deep breath, he jumped into the water.

The surface split around him, and cold water rushed over his head. The submarine was moving faster now that it had hit the deeper water around the Three Sisters. He was going to have to hurry. He kicked upward, swimming with difficulty. The chain was trying to pull him down onto the rocky bottom of the river.

He let it unwind, quick as he could.

The midget sub, which looked like a Japanese Type A Ko-hyoteki — of which only fifty had been built during World War II — was driven by a single propeller. It controlled its depth by adjusting its fins like a torpedo rather than by adjusting its buoyancy the way a full-sized sub would. But for its fins to be useful, the Ko-hyoteki's propeller would need to be turning.

Stop the propeller and the sub would sink.

He let the smooth dark side of the sub pass by underneath him. The weight of the chain seemed determined to drag him under. He had to expend most of his effort powerfully kicking his legs, just to keep his head above the water.

The aft end of the sub approached. Sam heaved the chain over the tail end of the hull, metal grinding against metal. The weight dragged the aft downward, aiming the forward end up. The flow of water over the sub's hull caused the chain to slide backward toward the propeller.

Sam kept the remaining end of the chain gripped in one hand. Now, he fed it into the blades of the propeller. At first nothing happened, and Sam began to swear. *Did I miss it completely?*

He was holding his breath, letting himself sink to the depth of the min-sub when he felt a tug on the chain. Obligingly, the blades caught the links and started to draw them back around the shaft.

The chain pulled smoothly for only a second.

Sam waited.

The chain caught against one of the blades and fouled around it, winding around the shaft. The propeller ground to a halt. Still straining to turn, the shaft started to leak dark oil into the water…

Sam kicked his legs hard, swimming away from the sub. A moment later he watched the craft start to sink. Without the forward momentum needed, it would soon be at the bottom of the deepest part of the Potomac, about eighty feet under at this point. After taking a few quick, deep breaths, he duck-dived, keeping his eyes on the submarine, until it finally reached the silty bed of the Potomac.

The hatch remained shut.

He waited as long as his lungs would allow him, and then swam back up to the surface. He didn't idle in the middle of the river. Instead, he rapidly stroked toward the shore.

Hypothetically, deep, fresh water should be able to insulate the populated area around them from radiation if the bomb went off. Unfortunately, the weapon's shockwave was still going to be lethal.

CHAPTER TEN

SAM SAT ON the edge of the east river bank panting raggedly.

A black helicopter hovered directly above where the sub had sunk in the Potomac. Its side doors swung open. Seven Navy SEAL divers stepped off the skids, dropping into the river, disappearing into the water below.

Sam watched as all but one of the elite team of Navy divers sank into the now murky water, while one of the men surface swam over to meet him.

The Navy diver came out of the water grinning. "My name's Lieutenant Worly. I'm here to make sure you're all right! Your crazy escapade to stop the submarine from continuing up the Potomac? It was genius! We spotted the sub inactive on the bottom of the river."

Sam's cheeks dimpled with amusement. "Hey, it worked, didn't it?"

Worly's smile disappeared. "We'll soon find out."

"Yeah, we will." Sam offered his right hand. "I'm Sam Reilly by the way."

Worly shook his hand with a firm shake, meeting his eyes. "It's a pleasure to meet you, Sam Reilly. No injuries?"

"None. Thanks, I'm fine."

"I've heard a lot about you."

"All good, I hope."

The diver shook his head and released Sam's hand. "Not *all* good."

Sam shrugged, indifferently. He'd been called names before. "What do you think? Will you be able to defuse it?"

"A nuclear bomb from the 1940s?" The diver cocked an eyebrow. "Hopefully. We won't know for sure until we open up that mini-sub and find out what type of arming plugs they were using."

"You don't know?" Sam asked, still catching his breath from his dive.

"No one knows. How could we? Until a few hours ago, no one had even heard of Germany successfully producing a nuclear weapon during WWII." The diver sighed. "We're hoping the arming plugs were based on similar technology to what the Manhattan Project developed during that period — but that's only a hope. In reality, there's every chance that the Germans came up with a different solution to simultaneous detonation."

Sam asked, "I was worried there was a risk of it being accidentally triggered by the sudden change in the sub's depth when I sank it. Apparently not."

The SEAL shook his head. "Where traditional bombs can be activated by any sudden change in movement, nuclear weapons take an extraordinary amount of effort to activate."

"A nearby explosion won't set off the reaction?" Sam asked.

"Not a chance. Do you know how a nuclear explosion works?"

Sam shook his head. "Not a clue. I must have been away from class the day they were teaching that in school."

The diver gave him a thin-lipped smile. "Basically. They work by simultaneously compressing the fissionable material — either enriched uranium 238 or plutonium 239 — to its critical mass."

"The weapon works on an implosion?"

"Exactly. Later they developed what is called a neutron

trigger — also known as a modulated neutron initiator — capable of producing a burst of neutrons on activation that would kick start the chain reaction of nuclear fission."

"But not in 1945?"

"No." The diver said, "I can't say for certain what the Germans had developed, but at Oak Ridge, the Manhattan Project built an exploding-bridgewire — EBW — a precision-timed detonator. It's used to initiate the explosion using an electric current, similar to a blasting cap, that precisely compresses the bomb's plutonium pit and initiates the reaction."

"How did they do that?"

"EBW detonators were typically constructed of either gold, platinum, or an alloy of the two, and are activated with the application of a strong electrical current — about 1000 amperes per microsecond–typically from a Marx generator. This powerful current heats the metal so quickly and in such a small area that the liquid vaporizes. A few nanoseconds after, the wire explodes, creating a shock wave and releasing the contained thermal energy, igniting the rest of the reaction."

"Interesting." Sam glanced at his watch. Nearly five minutes had passed since the rest of the SEAL team had disappeared beneath the surface of the Potomac. "As I'm fit and healthy, why are you still here?"

"I'm making sure you don't dive in for curiosity's sake." Then Worly gave a rueful smile. "Also, my wife just gave birth to a baby girl. That *might* have been the reason I got picked to keep you out of trouble."

"Congratulations," Sam said, bestowing a genuine smile. "Your first?"

"Yes, and it makes me doubly worry."

Sam frowned. He didn't know a lot about nuclear weapons, but he knew enough to realize they were well within the blast radius. "I don't expect that the bank of the Potomac is far enough away to keep either of us out of trouble..."

The diver shrugged philosophically. "Then my men will need to make sure the bomb doesn't get the chance to detonate."

They waited. With every minute that passed, Sam's jaw clinched harder.

Finally, a head broke the surface of the river, swimming over to the two of them. "Worly," the other man called. "We need your help down here, and we could use yours, too, Mr. Reilly. The mini-sub needs to be moved so we can get into it, we don't have enough manpower to do it on our own. We could either wait for a truck with a winch to get out here–"

"Or I could free-dive down with you and we can see if with more manpower we can push it ourselves," Sam said. "All right, let's do this."

Worly said, "You can buddy breathe from my regulator."

"Thanks."

Sam buddy-dived to the bottom with Worly.

The Potomac had silted up from the crash at the bottom as the current was a steady push from upstream. Sam free-dove downward. The midget sub was a dark shadow on the riverbed, he could almost have mistaken it for a rock.

The entrance to the sub was a hatch in the front of the finlike conn tower, and it was butted up against a solid piece of rock. Worly offered Sam his regulator, and he took a few breaths as he considered the situation. The divers were trying to roll the submarine off the rock. Rotating it would likely work better.

Sam swam to the aft end of the midget sub and started pulling the chain away from the propeller. He had no intention of unjamming it, only shifting the weight a little. He dropped the chain down into the silt at the bottom of the riverbed, then waved the other men over.

After a short, waved conference, the four men braced themselves and pulled on the chain. The conn tower caught against the rock, and as the aft end of the midget sub swung one way, the forward end swung the other. A few seconds later, the hatch was clear of the rock, with just enough room for a diver to maneuver.

Sam and Worly watched as the other divers prepared to enter.

The hatch was soon opened, and a pair of the divers slipped inside. For a couple of minutes, Sam had almost forgotten that their lives were at stake.

Now he remembered.

Soon one of the divers had emerged. He swam over to the two of them and waved them toward the hatch. Sam took another breath from the regulator, then swam inside.

The sub was cramped, but empty. No pilot.

No nuclear bomb.

The first diver waved toward Sam, then pointed to one of the inner walls. On it, written in diver's chalk, were the words:

Mr. Sam Reilly,

So good of you to join us. Now that you're here, the game can begin…

The message was unsigned.

CHAPTER ELEVEN

SAM SURFACED ALONGSIDE the other divers. This time, he emerged on the west side of the river. The Secretary of Defense was there, waiting for him, her helicopter waiting nearby.

"Well?" she asked.

"No bomb," Sam said. "The sub's empty."

She closed her eyes and exhaled a deep breath. Opening them again, she said, "Nothing there? Not even a pilot?"

Sam nodded. "Nothing except a note."

"A note?"

"Yeah, it was addressed to me specifically. Its author wrote: so good of you to join us. Now that you're here, the game can begin…"

Her jaw tightened with displeasure. "Someone's playing a game with you?'

"It would appear so, ma'am." Sam grimaced. "But even though the note was addressed to me, the game is being played with everybody—like it or not."

"Christ. Who knows how many powerful people you and your family have pissed off over the years?" She turned to an aide, and, taking command of the situation said, "I need a handwriting analyst, an underwater forensics team, and a terrorism profiler. This doesn't sound like the usual sort.

Nothing about religion or politics. We're going to have to bring that sub up, but I don't have time for it now. What the hell kind of terrorist wants to play a game with *you,* Reilly? This is going to be an absolute shit storm."

"I have to agree, ma'am." It was a sunny day, but someone thoughtfully dropped a blanket over his shoulders anyway. "I don't have a clue who's trying to get my attention, but I'm going to find out."

"How?"

He shrugged. "A little detective work. I think I'll start with the kid who inherited the map to the bomb."

The secretary shook her head. "I've already had him checked over. He's a nobody, Sam. You know what he's been doing since he got his inheritance? Spending it in Manhattan. Let me correct myself in case I gave you the wrong impression. He's bought an apartment building and appears to be setting it up as some kind of computer-game haven. Sound proof walls, energy drinks, and computer games. There's no way he could have retrieved the bomb. We have him under surveillance."

Sam asked, "You've checked with air traffic control for any flights during the last week between Maryland and the Great Falls of the Potomac?"

"Of course. We have no records of any helicopters or other craft flying near the crash area in the last three months. Nothing."

Sam watched the water. The other divers had come up. It was going to be impossible to move the midget sub out of the river until after the lockdown on D.C. ended. There was no way to get a vehicle into the area to pull the sub out, or to haul it away. As always during an emergency, everyone was trying to make an exception of themselves, and every road was packed bumper-to-bumper with cars. It was all the local police—already stretched beyond their limits—could do to keep the onlookers away from the riverbank.

Nothing to see here. Just a sub that might have been carrying a nuclear bomb...

"What are you thinking?" the secretary asked.

"Something is off about all this."

"Agreed. To what are you specifically referring? Anything? Or just a general sense?"

"Something specific is bothering me." As he spoke, the off feeling settled in his mind. "That bomb had to weigh, what? Several thousand pounds?"

The secretary shook her head. "My people tell me it would have weighed more in the vicinity of eleven thousand. Why?"

"It seems pretty much impossible to move a bomb weighing more than five and a half tons out of a thickly wooded area on foot. Or was there a road cut into the trees?"

"No, nothing like that. I've seen drone footage."

He grinned. "So how did they do it?"

"We've no idea."

"Maybe the question isn't how, but *when*. The bomb isn't here in the river *now*. Which means that it could have been moved earlier. Since we know the kid didn't do it, it doesn't even depend on him receiving his grandfather's bequest including the map. Anybody could have found it and moved it."

"Good point. I'll have the records search widened."

Sam looked back and forth between D.C. and the Virginia sides of the river. Traffic backed up as far as the eye could see. "I need a ride to Manhattan. I could call Tom to get me, but I don't think the Air Force would be too happy. This entire area must be a no-fly-zone."

"I can get you to the Ronald Reagan Airport. You can take a commercial jet to JFK."

"It's a deal. After that I'll pay the kid a visit and see what I can learn about his grandfather — and whoever else he might have spilled his secrets to."

"You still think he was involved?" the Secretary of Defense

asked.

He shrugged. "He's the only lead we've got."

Sam boarded the VH-60N Black Hawk with the Secretary of Defense, who needed to return to the Pentagon to update the President and the Commander of the Joint Chiefs of Staff — who were now bunkered beneath the White House.

Sam took his seat next to her, put his headset and seatbelts on, as the Black Hawk took off. It nosed down and began its south-eastern direction, crossing the Potomac, heading in a direct route to the Pentagon.

Behind them a second VIP helicopter was ferrying the first set of Congressmen and Congresswomen out of the Capitol.

Sam leaned back into his chair and exhaled a deep breath of air. Everything had happened so quickly in the past thirty minutes, it was hard to take it all in. He closed his eyes for a moment, then opened them again.

They were nearly across the Potomac.

The flash rose from the eastern side of the river — outside of the Capital — racing toward them.

He swore and an instant later, the pilot banked sharply to the left.

The FIM-92 Stinger's surface-to-air missile raced past them, leaving a trail of fire, locking onto the tail of the second helicopter.

Sam braced. His head snapped round, his eyes following the missile's deadly trajectory as it struck the tail of the second helicopter.

The tail erupted into a ball of flame and for a second the helicopter hovered, while the pilot tried to maintain control. Unbalanced, and unable to offset the extreme torque by the main rotor, the helicopter made progressively larger and larger circles before entering an uncontrollable spin.

The pilot throttled down and set the craft into autorotation.

Sam watched as the helicopter raced toward the surface of the

Potomac, before leveling out gradually an instant before it struck the surface of the river. The main rotor blade kept spinning, slicing the waves, before the helicopter sank, disappearing beneath the murky waters.

CHAPTER TWELVE

Sam felt his gut slide, as the pilot of the Secretary's Black Hawk increased speed and height. For a heated minute the helicopter raced along the Potomac before coming in to land on the secure helipad on top of the Pentagon.

As the rotor blades came to a dull whine the Secretary of Defense unclipped her harness and leaned toward the pilot. Her voice was loud and confident as she spoke, "Henriks! What do we know?"

The airman looked back at her, over his shoulder. "Not much I'm afraid, ma'am. Someone based on the east side of the Potomac fired a Stinger surface-to-air missile. It narrowly missed us, and took out our tailing helicopter from the 12th Aviation Battalion."

"Any survivors?"

"Yes. According to reports. Several occupants have surfaced and climbed on board a deployed life raft."

Her jaw set. "And the shooter or shooters?"

"At this time we believe there is only one. Teams are on the ground as we speak, attempting to locate."

Sam stood up and stared out the side windows toward the Potomac. From his vantage point on top of the Pentagon, his eyes swept the river, making out the small yellow shape of a life raft. They were slowly paddling to the western side.

The pilot switched the engine off, its rotor blades turned quietly.

The silence was interrupted by the echoing sounds of loud gunshots, firing in a rapid staccato. Sam squinted, fixing his eyes on the survivors. The sound seemed to be coming from there.

Bullets raked the surface of the river directly in front of the life raft.

Congressmen, Congresswomen, and servicemen jumped back into the water.

The shots ceased.

Why had the sharp shooter stop firing?

One of the Congressmen immediately began swimming toward the western side of the river. He made it nearly fifteen feet before the gunman began firing his rifle once more.

Sam quickly picked up a pair of binoculars hanging on the inside of the helicopter—normally used for sightseeing VIPs on their flight over the Capitol. Adjusting the instrument for his vision, he studied the river.

"Christ almighty!" Sam swore. "I get it. Someone's trying to make certain no one leaves the Capitol."

"You have to be kidding me!" The Secretary of Defense fixed her emerald eyes on the river as the scene unfolded. "Then why don't they head to the east side, for goodness sakes?"

Another bullet struck the water, missing a man in a suit by no more than a foot. That settled it for the survivors. They turned and started swimming toward the east side. The shots immediately ceased.

"There they go," Sam said.

"Sure. But now it's obvious the terrorist intends to keep them on that side of the river."

Sam's wry voice carried a cheerful note, "Yeah, but at least we know his intention isn't to intentionally kill anyone. Not yet, at any rate."

In the silence a cell phone started to ring from up front.

The pilot looked back at Sam. "Hey, I think that's your phone."

The Secretary of Defense passed his cell back to him.

He answered it. "Hello?"

"Sam Reilly?" The voice was garbled by a voice-scrambler.

"Speaking," Sam replied, turning his cell onto speaker mode and gesturing to the Secretary of Defense to listen. "What can I do for you?"

"Right now, all I want you to do is pass a message onto the good-looking redhead next to you."

Sam's pulse skipped as he scanned the area around him. The terrorist, whoever he or she was, had eyes on him and was close enough to know exactly who he was with. "Okay. What's the message?"

"No one but you comes in or out of the capital. The German nuclear bomb is hidden within the capital. If you play the game correctly everyone gets to go home. If you break any of the rules, it's game over and I detonate the bomb."

"What are the rules?" Sam asked.

"No one from Congress leaves the capital. My teams have surrounded the perimeter of the city, the edge of the Potomac, and the Anacostia. If I see special forces from the police or military encroach on these positions a lot of people will die. No air traffic anywhere in the city."

"Okay. I'll pass the message on." Sam noted a slight flickering of sunlight coming from the edge of the Potomac and wondered if it was their attacker. "What do you want from me?"

"Your participation."

"In what?"

"A game. A contest. Winner takes all."

Sam squinted, trying to see if he could get a better view of the man. "Okay. Sure. How do I play?"

"You're about to make your first move." A series of bombs went off along K street NW, 11th Street NW, and Rhode Island Avenue NW, effectively cutting the capital in two. "There. I've made the game board smaller. I'm only interested in those to the south of that line. I'm afraid I'm going to be busy for a while now, but I'll let you know when it's time for you to make your next move."

Sam stared at the series of fires that split the capital in half. He turned to face the Secretary of Defense. "What are you going to do?"

Exiting the helicopter, she picked up her secure satellite phone. Sam followed her lead, as did the pilot. "First, I'm going to make a call to ensure the police and special forces keep back from the city's perimeter, the edge of the Potomac, and the Anacostia. I'm also going to put a stop on air traffic."

The Secretary made her calls as she walked.

The two of them strode into an elevator. "Now, I'm going to inform the President of our situation. He has advisors who will want to consider the next steps to take." Her piercing green eyes fixed on him. "The question is, Mr. Reilly, why in hell does this terrorist want to play a game with you? More importantly, what are you going to do about it?"

Sam shrugged. "I have no idea why he picked me. But for now, I'm going to catch a flight to New York to see that kid. I'll get my people to find out everything they can about his grandfather. We'll find a connection."

"Is that the wisest thing to do?" Her eyebrows narrowed. "I mean, given that this extremist wants to play this game with you specifically?"

"He didn't say not to go anywhere. Besides, he said he would be busy for a while."

"In that case, I'd better organize a military jet to take you to NY. That way you're no more than an hour away. I want you close, just in case the man with his finger on the button wants to contact you again."

CHAPTER THIRTEEN

MANHATTAN, NEW YORK

ALEX GOODSON STRUCK Sam as being the kind of guy who was book smart but lacking in any sort of social or street sense. Yet, he wasn't exactly stupid in that way, either. Instead, Sam noticed the young man was trying to be something that he was not. Looking around the place, it appeared more like Goodson didn't seem to be able to connect his intelligence to anything useful.

For example, the building that Goodson had bought in Manhattan, a four-story brick walkup with a cell phone retailer and an internet service provider at the bottom, was rocking a twenty-four-hour gaming party when Sam reached it.

When he introduced himself, Goodson shrugged. "It's not my fault that those treasure hunters caused so much trouble, okay? I didn't have anything to do with that."

Sam stopped himself from gaping at the kid. Of course Goodson, and nobody else, was responsible for posting the map online. This had directly led to the swarm of treasure hunters that had swarmed the area right afterward.

The kid's reaction showed such a profound lack of insight into the situation that Sam had to take a mental step back and start over.

"Hi," he said. "My name's Sam Reilly. I've been sent by the Secretary of Defense to try to sort through the information that your grandfather left you. We need to find out who might have taken the bomb that was on that plane."

"You didn't find it?" Alex asked, opening a beer fridge full of energy drinks and soft drinks. "Jeez. That's not good." He opened his soda, a can of Dr. Pepper. "You want one?"

Sam restrained a grimace. "No thanks. Can I see the note your grandfather left you?" The FBI and the CIA had made copies, and had already gone through everything in the kid's apartment. It didn't seem to have bothered him.

Alex said, "Hang on a sec." He left Sam on the second-floor landing. Except for the commercial spaces on the ground floor, the other tenants in the building appeared to have been evicted — or bribed to leave, probably. Workmen were carrying out their possessions: mattresses, shelving units, pet carriers, boxes that clinked as they were carried. The blaring music suddenly stopped. Someone was using a power drill on one of the floors above.

"The stuff the government guys went through is up on the fourth floor," Alex shouted from somewhere in the apartment building. "Head on up. I'll meet you in a sec."

Sam climbed the two flights of stairs. From what he could see of the landings, the apartments were being stripped out and turned into server rooms.

A moment later, the kid entered the room, holding a beer. "Here, I thought you might need this. You look like you've had a pretty crappy day."

Sam shook his head. "Thanks. But I kind of need my wits about me right now. I think one of those might just put me to sleep. I'd be better off with a coffee or a stimulant."

"I can get you one of those, too."

"You have coffee?" Sam asked.

"No. But I've got a fridge full of energy drinks."

"No thanks." Sam grimaced again. His eyes swept the array of fiber optic cabling being routed throughout the stairwell. "What are you setting up in here?"

"Oh, just a gamer's paradise." Alex grinned. "Me and some friends of mine have had this on a 'someday if I win the lottery' wish list for years. High-end systems all networked together, games already installed, tech support on hand. We're going to have a tournament as soon as I can get everything set up in here. It's gonna be awesome!"

Alex was tall, skinny, pale, and his face had been ravaged by acne. A typical basement-dweller, he seemed a combination of smart and stupid, with two left feet. Friendly enough, he was the kind of guy who'd probably never been on a date. The kind of guy who got left behind in a world full of adults. There was something else there, too. Sam blinked.

Behind his bumbling exterior, Sam was certain the kid's pale gray eyes were sharp and filled with intelligence.

Was it all a show? Could Alex really be intelligent enough to fake everything?

Sam patted him on his shoulder. "I'm sure it'll be a lot of fun. Where would I find your grandfather's things?"

Sam watched, but Alex didn't flinch or seem to respond negatively to the paternalistic gesture.

"Oh, sure. Follow me."

Alex led him to the rearmost apartment, which had been left more or less intact. A tiny, galley-style kitchen, a bathroom with about six square inches of open space to stand in, a bedroom stuffed with a modest full-sized bed. The sofa was ratty but the television had been upgraded to the point that it reminded him of the military command wall screens found at some military installations he'd been to.

Alex left Sam at the café-sized kitchen table with an archive box full of paperwork.

"This is all Grandpa's stuff," he said, then walked into the living room and switched on the TV. In a few moments, he was playing some kind of video game with a set of headphones on, the least concerned guy in the world.

The fact that millions of people could have died today because of his carelessness seemed to have completely escaped him.

Sam shook his head and started going through the box that probably fifty government agents had already pawed through.

CHAPTER FOURTEEN

Sam read through the old papers and journals for a couple hours.

What he learned was that William Goodson had been an interesting character, far more driven and purposeful than his grandson. Reading through newspaper clippings, the man appeared to be an all-American hero. He had flown bomber planes during the Korean War, worked for Lockheed-Martin for a number of years, then shifted to piloting commercial jets for American Airlines. He had kept records showing his donations to several charities and his church. He had retired from his position on the advisory board a few years before his death nearly a decade ago and had rented the very same apartment that Sam was sitting in now. This stirred Sam's inner alarms a little, but he couldn't quite put a finger on why.

Most of the records that were in the box pointed toward a normal, everyday life. The life of an ordinary man who had left Germany in the 1940s after World War II, married, had a son, lost his wife in 1995, and watched his grandson grow up. Then he had died. More than a decade later, when his own son had died, he left millions to his grandson.

Where had William Goodson's generous largess come from?

Had Grandpa Goodson and Alex's father quarreled or something? Why didn't the man simply impart his massive wealth to his own son? Why wait until his son had died to bequeath his wealth to his grandson?

The Secretary of Defense might have well been right. It appeared that Alex Goodson didn't have anything to do with the terrorist threat to Washington, D.C. Yet there was no doubt in Sam's mind that everything about Alex and his inheritance led to more questions than answers.

He picked up an old photo of William Goodson. There was no question of familial connection. The two men could be the same person, separated by about seventy years. He pictured Alex dressed up in an old American Airlines pilot's uniform.

Sam's ocean blue eyes fixed on William Goodson's gray eyes, strong jaw line, and rigid expression.

Who were you, really?

The man had turned out to be a World War II German bomber pilot carrying a fake passport, who had crashed. Unable to carry out his mission, William Goodman had assimilated seamlessly into the country he had come to destroy.

It was almost as if he had had a change of heart.

Settling in America, he had put down roots after falling in love with a local girl. Margery Pull had a sweet, kind face and worked as a schoolteacher until her marriage.

Sam took another look around the living area. Neither lavish nor stingy, it wasn't the apartment of a multi-millionaire or a miser. The yellow enamel sink was worn and chipped, but it was clean.

He stood up and stretched.

The kid glanced over at him, paused his video game, and pulled his headphones off.

"Find what you needed?"

"Alex, if it's not too personal—I don't see anything in here that explains how your grandfather became a millionaire."

"I know, right?" Alex grinned. "I had no idea. I don't think Dad did, either. Grandpa was always complaining about me not getting a job because nobody was going to take care of me when he was gone."

"So where do you think it came from?"

"German relatives. He inherited the money back in the forties, mostly. I guess Germany was pretty much in an uproar at the time, so he was lucky to get anything at all. But the money was in Swiss bank accounts, so the Germans couldn't touch it. That's what I'm guessing anyway. The money's been sitting in a local bank for nearly eight decades."

Sam sighed. Money hit some people in strange ways. He'd grown up around it all his life, tended not to think about it — but some people became obsessed with it. William Goodson didn't seem to fit in that category. If anything, it looked as though the man had simply stored the money away in a bank for safekeeping and lived off the ordinary wage that he'd earned.

None of it made sense, even if Sam believed the story about rich, dead German relatives. Still, it was most likely cash the Reich had put into an account for his grandfather as incentive to blow up D.C.

No need to tell the strange, backward kid that, though. Let him have his fun.

Sam left his cell phone number with Alex. "If you can think of anything at all that might help, give me a call."

"Sure."

Thirty seconds later, the kid was back in front of the hundred-and-ten-inch TV with his headphones on.

Sam shook his head and watched the game for a few minutes. It looked like one of those real time strategy games, set in some sort of urban warzone. It was from the perspective of the characters on the ground. He couldn't see very much of the surrounding city, but it could be set in any modern civilization around the world — possibly even in the U.S.

He watched as Alex selected various soldiers in black balaclavas and tasked them to guard or secure various locations. The place looked familiar, but he couldn't quite place it. In the background there was a hot air blimp. It was tethered to a rope above a building, with a large advertisement for some local law firm.

Alex suddenly noticed Sam's interest. He paused the game again. "Hey, you wanna play a game?"

"What?" Sam thought he misheard the kid.

"You wanna play a game with me?"

"No, thanks." Sam lips curled into an incredulous grin, revealing a small dimple to his cheek. "Um… maybe another time. I'm a little busy right now."

"Oh, yeah, what with?" Alex asked.

Sam shook his head. *Was this kid for real?* "There's a terrorist attack on our nation's capital."

Alex stood up and grinned, making a poor attempt at feigning embarrassment. "Oh right, of course. I forgot. Just remember, I offered to let you play my game instead. I think you'd find it a little more fun."

Sam felt like hitting the kid, but it was obvious that it wouldn't help. As bright as the man might be, he wasn't synapsing the way normal individuals should. Perhaps it was better Alex should lock himself in a gaming room, away from the rest of the world.

He stood up to leave.

"Remember what I said, if you can think of anything about your grandfather that might help, please give me a call."

Alex nodded. "Will do. Good luck with your game."

Sam paused. "What did you say?"

"Good luck with your game."

"I'm not playing any silly computer game here. Don't you understand, this is real? I'm trying to stop a madman with a nuclear bomb from destroying our capital and everything good that stands for democracy."

Alex appeared unfazed by the reproach. He made what

appeared to be a genuine smile. Despite the small scars of his once pockmarked face, the kid would have been considered handsome. "I know."

"Good."

A wry smile and mischievous look formed on Alex's face. "I hope you win, Mr. Reilly."

CHAPTER FIFTEEN

SAM STEPPED OUT of the front door of Alex's apartment. He glanced out at his ride and the uniformed officer who was waiting to take him back to JFK airport. Taking two steps at a time, he reached the third set of landing steps, when his cell phone rang.

He picked it up on the first ring. "Sam, speaking."

"You were right," was the first thing the Secretary of Defense said.

It was unusual for her to give an inch. The small crease of a smile formed across his face. "Thanks. I thought I was, but what about?"

"The bomb wasn't moved out of that wooded area in the last week or even the last month."

"How far back did you have to go?" Sam asked.

"Five years."

In other words, after Grandpa William Goodson's passing — but long before the death of Alex Goodson's father. "That had to be from satellite records, right? That was fast."

"We have some very patient people working for us, and some very good computer algorithms."

"And?" he asked.

"And the empty casing for the bomb was already outside the downed aircraft." The Secretary sighed heavily. "Actually, not just outside of it, but outside of the mine shaft. It's left laying on the surface nearby, intermingled with the rest of the dilapidating mining equipment from the late 1930s."

"Wait—you didn't mention that before."

"Yes. The bomb's outer shell had been removed from the plane, and left outside the mine shaft's entrance. Yet it was still within the National Park Service fences which were put in place more than twenty years ago to preserve the historic Maryland Mine Company's abandoned gold mine."

"The site can be seen by tourists?" Sam asked.

"Sure, there's a dedicated Gold Mine Loop trail through the historic Maryland Mine Ruins, why?"

"Then, why hasn't anyone ever noticed the bomb casing before?"

"Bad luck on our part I guess. People just didn't know what they were looking at. It's not surprising given the fenced area included the dilapidated remains of an old water tank, blacksmith shop, and overgrown sealed shaft entrances."

"All right," Sam said, shaking his head. "When was the bomb removed from the plane?"

The secretary repeated, "The empty casing was already outside the aircraft as of five years ago."

"Did you find anything earlier?"

"Not yet. We're still searching."

"Then the bomb could have been taken even before then. Say as far back as during William Goodson's lifetime. He might've removed it in the forties. This could all be some kind of post-death plot of Goodson's to destroy D.C., for all we know."

"Exactly." That seemed to trigger the Secretary of Defense's memory. "What about you, Sam? Did you find anything from Alex Goodson?"

Sam said, "I don't know. You're right, Alex probably isn't involved in this–"

"But?"

"But he's not who he's pretending to be, either," Sam said.

"Which makes me wonder, why?"

"All right, we'll keep our surveillance on him," The Secretary said. "He tries to leave his apartment we'll know."

Sam asked, "Where are you with the situation in D.C., ma'am?"

"We have more than a dozen teams from the FBI, CIA, and the Military who have worked there way around the perimeter. Right now, a Major Kyle Ortega and his team from the 832nd Ordnance Battalion out of Fort Lee is heading up the mission to retrieve and disarm the nuclear bomb — as soon as its located."

"Are they going to enter the capital?" Sam asked.

"Not yet. Our reconnaissance shows that the terrorist has at least three hundred ground troops, guarding the perimeter. They're covered in dark military attire and balaclavas, but are equipped with state of the art military weapons, including multiple shoulder mounted Stingers that they used to take out the helicopter previously."

"Three hundred sounds like a fairly small number to maintain control of the perimeter of Washington, D.C.," Sam said. "Surely our tactical teams can force their penetration into the city without too much trouble?"

"Of course they can, but that doesn't change the primary fact that our madman may still be willing to detonate a nuclear bomb."

Sam swallowed hard and his back made an involuntary shudder. "What do you need me to do, ma'am?"

"Play the terrorist's stupid game," the Secretary commanded. "Keep him distracted until we can locate the bomb and end this thing."

"Understood."

"And, Mr. Reilly."

"Yes, ma'am."

"For God's sake, don't antagonize our terrorist any more than you already have."

CHAPTER SIXTEEN

SAM CLIMBED INTO the Ford Taurus AWD Interceptor and the NY Highway Patrol Officer who'd been assigned to expedite his trip back, drove him to JFK airport.

He flicked through his cell phone and called a number. The receiver answered on the first ring. Ordinarily, there's risk involved in using an open, insecure wireless network, but his people had taken every step to safeguard his phone. Even better, the woman he was about to call was even more stringently careful with security.

"Elise," Sam said, as the big Ford Taurus accelerated through NY city traffic. "I need your help."

"Of course, you do," she said. "What do you need?"

"Where are you?" he asked.

"Does it matter? Within arm's reach of more processing power than the U.S. Government will admit exists outside its own server banks."

Sam shook his head. Elise was a brilliant young computer geek who had been raised as some kind of secret hacker weapon for the CIA, only to thumb her nose at the position. She was sharp enough to make it stick, too.

"Good, you're going to need it."

He explained the situation briefly, touching on the bomb, the crash site, Alex Goodson's father's death and his unexpected inheritance from his grandfather. He detailed posting the map, the treasure hunters, the mini-sub, the message within, and his recent visit to Alex Goodson's gamer's paradise.

"And?" she said finally. "You want me to hack into Alex Goodson's computer servers and see what games he's playing?"

"Yes, but I also need you to find out if there is a connection between William Goodson and my family."

"You think your dad might be involved in something he shouldn't be?"

Sam made a slight grimace. His father, Senator James Reilly, was smart yet single-minded in the games he played. He considered that the most important thing in life was to rack up more points than anyone else—the points in this case meaning accumulated wealth. "This does kind of sound like the thing he might somehow be involved in, doesn't it?"

"No comment. I'll check on the Goodson family."

"And I'll call my father."

He ended the call and searched his cell phone directory for his dad's number. Finding it a moment later, he pressed the call button.

"Son," James Reilly said in a warm, appreciative tone. "What's going on? D.C.'s on lockdown and Tom Bower says that you left for Reagan National Airport like a bat out of hell a few hours ago."

"Dad," Sam said, "I don't have time to explain."

"And?"

"And I need to know if you're involved in something before I tear it wide open."

Sam heard a soft *hmm* over the phone. "You're starting to think like a politician, Sam. I'm proud of you."

Sam wasn't sure he wanted to take that as a compliment. "Never mind that. What do you know about William Goodson?"

"Who?"

"World War II, German bomber pilot, originally named Wilhelm Gutwein."

"Nothing."

"And you're not involved in anything having to do with a nuclear bomb found in an old gold mine site along the Great Falls of the Potomac?"

"You found a nuclear bomb within the Maryland National Park?" James gasped incredulously. The shocked tone in his father's voice told him everything he needed to know.

"Thanks, Dad. Call you back soon with more information. Bye."

He put his phone in his pocket and chuckled. It wasn't every day he was able to surprise his old man.

CHAPTER SEVENTEEN

ELISE CALLED BACK a few minutes later. "There's nothing. At least nothing that was ever documented anywhere."

Sam cursed under his breath. "You're sure?"

"Lots of information but nothing that connects the Goodson's to the Reilly clan."

"For example?"

"The Gutwein family was from Kassel, in west-central Germany. Loads of industrial sites there. They made tanks and planes and train engines. Consequently, the place was bombed for three years straight."

"Go on."

"Except for Wilhelm Gutwein, the entire family was killed during a British bombing raid in October of 1943. All burned to death in a firestorm of exploding fuel."

"Losing your family is a hell of a motive. It certainly explains why Goodson agreed to bomb D.C."

"True, but the original attack wasn't simply revenge. This was Germany's last chance at winning the war—or at least not losing it."

"Sure. Even so, it doesn't tell me why he's targeting me."

"Nope. Unless it has nothing to do with the Goodson/Gutwein family, and it's one of the many, many other people that you've pissed off over the years."

"I don't know, Elise. This sounded kind of personal."

She sighed. "Um… what I said. All right, I'll keep on it."

The Highway Patrol car pulled into the private terminal at JFK. The place was used by wealthy business people, whose private jets were waiting for them to arrive. In this case, a military jet was waiting to transfer Sam back to Ronald Reagan airport.

Sam thanked the Officer and closed the door.

Immediately afterward, his cell phone started to ring. He glanced at the screen — it was an unlisted number.

He answered it.

"Sam Reilly," he answered, scanning the high-rise buildings of Manhattan in the distance. "Who is this?"

"Someone who'd like to play a little game with you."

From the first word, Sam knew who it was — in theory, anyway. The voice had been garbled by a voice-scrambler.

The bad guy — if it was indeed a guy — was about to make another move.

Elise had set up his phone with a menu of high-tech tricks years ago. Sam now punched in the code that activated a voice recorder and flagged Elise's systems to start tracing the call.

"All right," Sam said. "I'm ready to play."

CHAPTER EIGHTEEN

"Good," replied the garbled voice. "But I'm going to need you to prove it."

Sam looked around. His aircraft was waiting on the tarmac. "All right. How?"

"Your cell phone, Mr. Reilly. It has to go."

"Okay. I'll drop it in a trash can."

"No. I'm watching. Hold it out directly in front of you."

Sam looked around, then stiff-armed, he did as he was told.

With a whizzing sound, a bicycle courier raced by—snatching the phone out of Sam's right hand.

Sam stood up and started running after the guy. The back of the messenger's shirt read *VELO COURIERS*. Within less than a minute, the guy had disappeared around a corner. Sam dodged pedestrians on the sidewalk, ducking into traffic when he could.

But by the time he reached the corner, the courier was long gone.

Clever.

Sam turned around, only to bump into a guy in a red polo shirt wearing a matching red hat.

"Sam Reilly?" the stranger asked.

"Yes."

"Your order." A plastic bag was shoved into Sam's hands.

The guy turned around and dodged his way across the sidewalk to the front of a sandwich shop.

Carl's Hoagies.

Checking inside the bag, Sam found it contained a well-wrapped long roll filled with chicken, cheese, and salad—and a phone in a freezer baggie. The sandwich was still warm.

He pulled out the cell as he pushed his way through the crowds toward the sub shop.

As soon as he entered the shop, he froze.

The staff here didn't wear red shirts and hats. They wore green with *Carl's Hoagies* embroidered on the caps.

"Did a guy in a red shirt and hat just buy a sandwich here?"

"Sure," said the middle age woman at the counter.

"Did you happen to get his name?"

"No."

"Do you have a record of his card transaction?" Sam asked, feeling hopeful.

"Paid cash." The cashier frowned. "What's this about?"

"Oh, he dropped his sandwich and left his cell phone in the bag," Sam said.

The woman squinted at him. Sam held up the clear bag containing the phone.

"That's weird."

"Here's my number, in case he shows up." Sam gave her Elise's number. He didn't expect to get a call, but it was better to have all bases covered.

On the way out of the shop, Sam's newly acquired phone rang. He answered. "Hello?"

The distorted voice spoke again. "Don't bother—they don't know anything. And even if you did find the guy, he wouldn't talk. He doesn't know what's going on, anyway. All he knows is that he won't get paid if he tells anyone about the job."

Sam said, "You mentioned something about playing a

game?"

"That's right. Think of it as a treasure hunt with a nice fat payoff at the end. Only you'll have to hurry. Because if you don't find that nuclear bomb in the next twenty-four hours, it's going to detonate. Then that will be the end of Washington, D.C."

The voice paused, giving Sam far too much time for his mind to conjure up Hiroshima-like images of American's capital.

"No one crosses the Beltway from here on out but you, Sam Reilly," the scrambled voice commanded. "No one in, and no one out. Once you're across the Beltway, I'll text you with your next set of instructions. You are not allowed to contact anyone. You are not free to accept anyone's help. Is that clear?"

"Yes."

"Then get started. Because you can't win if you don't play — and the lives of roughly a million people are at stake. You'd better hurry."

CHAPTER NINETEEN

I<small>T WAS ALL</small> over the news. *Terrorist attack on Washington, D.C.* The lockdown that the Secretary of Defense had implemented was expanded to cover additional territory, and was tightened even further. Now, even the military, police, and emergency transportation were shut down.

Sam was going to need some kind of assistance to get from Manhattan to D.C., no matter what the bad guy said. Walking the entire way was not an option. He needed transport.

Sam took the return military flight from JFK Airport to the Ronald Reagan airport just outside the Beltway, then he attempted to hire a Cessna 152 to fly himself into D.C.

The pilot stared at him wide-eyed. "You can't fly into D.C. It's on lockdown. Don't you know about the terrorist attack? Anyone who goes in or out of the area will trigger a nuclear bomb."

Sam started to explain, but didn't get very far before he was interrupted by the man's phone ringing.

"Hold on, I have to get this. It's my wife—"

When he answered the phone, his eyes nearly bugged out of his head. He turned toward Sam and his jaw dropped.

"Yes, sir," he said, all the color leaving his face. "Yes, sir."

He ended the call, automatically shoving the phone back into the pocket of his overalls. "That was the terrorist, Mr. Reilly," he said breathlessly, "calling on my wife's phone! I have to fly you anywhere you want to go or he'll hurt my wife!"

"Calm down. Your wife will be okay," Sam said, gripping the agitated man by the shoulder. "What else did he say?"

"You have his permission to fly directly into D.C.," he said, his voice calming. "I'm supposed to take you. And Mr. Reilly? He says I'm to land on the National Mall!"

CHAPTER TWENTY

THE SMALL AIRCRAFT was barely off the ground, before the pilot dipped its nose, leveling its climb angle to straight and level. It was going to be one hell of a short flight. The single engine changed its pitch, and the pilot commenced their descent.

The long, grassy National Mall is home to the Lincoln Memorial and the Washington Monument. At the eastern end is the domed U.S. Capitol. The White House is to the north. It's also flanked by Smithsonian museums.

Usually, the National Mall's lawns and pathways are crowded with school groups, softball teams, and joggers. Sam doubted anyone would be out enjoying their soon-to-be landing strip today.

The Cessna 152 flew over the Potomac, where it combined with the Anacostia.

Sam ran his eyes across the landscape below. Armed men — soldier, mercenaries, and terrorists — lined the river, and urban perimeter of the city. Rubble and the smoldering remains to the north outlined where a series of bombs went off along K street NW, 11th Street NW, and Rhode Island Avenue NW, effectively cutting the capital in two. On the outer side of the perimeter, a large convoy of battle tanks, armored personnel carriers, and ground troops took their respective positions along bridges and street blocks in preparation for storming the capital.

America's capital.

The sight took his breath away. His eyes turned to the domed Capitol building, across to the camouflaged mercenaries who now occupied it. His response was visceral. A beacon of democracy being ravaged by war and terrorism.

The engine went nearly silent, as the pilot reduced its RPM right back in preparation for landing. "I'm starting our descent."

Sam withdrew from his emotional response, instead focusing on the task at hand. "Understood."

Air traffic control must have been contacted by the terrorist as worried voices directed the Cessna's pilot to the Capitol. Directly over the Capitol Building they began their final descent, passing low and slowly flying mere feet over the cars jamming the streets.

They came down directly on the grass strip in the center of the mall. The back of the plane fishtailed as they came down and started sliding over the wet grass. Behind them they had left a long streak in the grass, with dark patches where the sod had been torn free.

Once the plane came to a stop, the pilot turned off the engine. "I'm not ashamed to say that I'm shaking like a leaf," he said.

Sam's phone buzzed, the signal that he'd just received a text message. The message led to the "Space Race" exhibit in the National Air and Space Museum.

Which was just past the cherry trees to his left.

It was clear to Sam that the mastermind behind this "game" had planned everything down to the inch. With a sigh, he climbed out of the plane.

"Hey, wait," the pilot called.

"Yes?"

"What am I supposed to do now?"

Sam gave him Tom Bower's number. "Call this number and tell Tom that you need a place to ride out the storm in D.C."

"Thanks."

Sam's phone buzzed again. This time the text said, *Don't try to get clever. I'm watching you.*

"Watch away," Sam muttered under his breath.

Once inside the Air and Space Museum, Sam took a look around. The museum was more or less abandoned, for now at least. If people were trapped in D.C. for long enough, they'd probably flood the place looking for something to do — or a place to spend the night. The hotels inside the Beltway were expensive and jam-packed at the best of times. No doubt they were already jacking up their prices for the night.

Now what?

No doubt his game-playing extremist had arranged his next step.

Sam was met at the doors of the museum by a pair of guards and escorted inside. Approaching him at a moderate walk was a wizened, white-haired man in a black suit with a striped tie and a mischievous smile. He was followed by a middle-aged woman in a brown pantsuit with a kind, round face. A cheerful golden scarf was tied around her neck, in contrast to her dark brunette hair.

The man's handshake was firm and emphatic. "Roger Nelson, Director of the National Air and Space Museum. This is Marge Toben, my assistant."

"Sam Reilly."

His assistant gave Sam a faint, uncertain smile but said nothing as she shook his hand more gently.

The main hall was scattered with exhibits both on the floor and overhead. *The Spirit of St. Louis,* flown by Charles Lindbergh, hung near the orange "Glamorous Glennis" Bell X-1, the first aircraft to break the sound barrier. The rest of the exhibits in the room were hardly less impressive. Overhead, the bright blue sky seemed to call the aircraft to come out and play.

Nelson winked. "I met your grandfather a time or two, back in the day."

The director's comment would ordinarily be of interest to Sam. Today, he could barely register what the man was saying. He was supposed to be on a "treasure hunt," but he had no idea what exactly he was looking for or where to start.

"Mr. Nelson, I hate to be so direct, but do you have any idea what I'm supposed to be doing here?"

"Not the slightest." The idea didn't seem to worry Nelson much. And yet Sam didn't get the sense that the man was a mental lightweight.

"Aren't you afraid of getting nuked?"

Nelson grimaced comically. "Son, I've lived under the threat of all kinds of bombs going off around me for longer than you and your father have been alive. Of course, I'm concerned. But afraid? No. My grandchildren and great-grandchildren all live on the other coast. They'll be fine, that's what's most important to me."

Behind him, the expression on Marge Toben's face looked pained. She rolled her eyes and shook her head. Sam decided to let it go and move on with more important matters.

In order to be able to act, Sam needed to gather more information. He needed to keep the terrorist placated by pretending to go through the motions of the treasure hunt—but he also needed to find a way to thwart the mastermind's plans, and he couldn't do that by just playing along.

He checked his phone again, hoping that he'd missed another text message, but no such luck.

"What's the exhibit that's been changed most recently?" he asked. Sam felt the madman had been making plans over at least the last five years, so any clues that he'd left would risk being spotted if he'd left them alone for too long.

"Why, our latest big overhaul was in *this* room, Mr. Reilly. We took down the planes and—"

"–I'm sorry, Director, but that was two years ago," Ms. Toben interrupted him. "The most recent display is in the Special

Exhibits Gallery, which is updated on a regular basis. It covers the early days of the Atomic Age, from Soddy and Rutherford in 1901 to the Manhattan Project, the Cold War, and–" Her brown eyes met his, questioningly, "Yes?"

"Heisenberg," Sam said.

"Yes, of course," Ms. Toben said. "We mention the Uranium club, the Alsos Mission, and more."

"Take me there, quickly. Right now!"

Ms. Toben received a thoughtful nod of approval from Director Nelson. Then she slipped off her high-heeled shoes, and started running down the hall with Sam in tow.

CHAPTER TWENTY-ONE

THE EXHIBIT HELD a replica of *Fat Man,* or Mark-III atomic bomb, in yellow and black. The enormous bomb stood as high as a man and had been painted disturbingly like a famous cartoon character's yellow-and-black shirt—due to the black liquid asphalt that had been sprayed over the bomb casing's seams. A Mark-36 bomb casing from the 1950s, green and yellow, sat nearby. Advertising materials for *Atomic Energy and You,* paper dolls in a paper fallout shelter, an *Atomic Chief* badge and mask, and more were displayed around the room.

"It's something in this room," Sam said.

Ms. Toben turned around slowly in a circle, blowing a tense breath from her pink cheeks. "I've looked over everything in the room so often that it looks more like interior décor than history."

One of the displays caught his eye, a model of an early nuclear pile surrounded by miniature figures of the scientists who had worked on it. Something about it called to him. He walked toward it with his hands deep in his pants pockets.

"What in the world?" Ms. Toben strode past him, reaching the display before him. The exhibit was set on a broad, open table covered by a chest-high acrylic shield. Without hesitation, she climbed up on the edge of the table and stepped over the acrylic shield. It made her look like the Atomic Woman.

"Make sure you don't disturb anything. It might be important."

"I won't."

"This is a model of the Chicago Pile-One, the earliest working nuclear reactor pile," Ms. Toben said, squatting over the display. "What on earth is this man doing in here?"

She pulled a foam-core, printed black-and-white model of a man off the floor of the display, squinting at it.

Sam recognized the man's features. Light-colored eyes that sparkled with humor, a long nose, high forehead, thin lips.

Werner Heisenberg.

"Oh!" Ms. Toben seemed to recognize him at the same time.

Referring to Heisenberg's uncertainty principle of being unable to measure an object's position and velocity at the same time with absolute accuracy, she said drily, "It seems we have lost the ability to track Mr. Heisenberg's location within this museum. He's not even supposed to have a figurine in this exhibit."

Surprising himself, Sam laughed at her joke. "Where do you think it came from?"

"Until we can review the security tapes, your guess is as good as mine."

Sam helped Ms. Toben climb safely back out of the exhibit, then held out a hand for the figurine.

"It looks like one of the well-known photographs of the man. I wonder if anything else in the exhibit changed?"

"May I please have a look?" he asked.

"By all means," she said, handing him the model.

Sam carefully studied the small plastic figurine. Despite its likeness to Werner Heisenberg, it could have been a kid's toy. Its weight suggested it was made entirely of plastic — there were no electronic parts or mechanical pieces that might hold some sort of hidden code or message. Sam pocketed the toy and continued reviewing the exhibit.

Director Nelson arrived and joined the search, circling the

room, examining each section of the display closely. Sam found himself staring at the text of a short article. It was posted on the wall under a photograph of what looked like another nuclear pile on the aborted German nuclear project known as the Uranium Club.

> *In 1943, the first working nuclear fission bomb was produced at Haigerloch, whimsically named "Die Koloratursoubrette," after a class of operatic soprano. The bomb was never used, nor tested. It was lost during Operation BIG in 1945, in which American teams captured or destroyed much of the information related to Germany's nuclear fission program, in which a peaceful agenda was its stated purpose.*

"So, the Haigerloch Research Reactor was actually used to construct a bomb," Sam said, reading the text. "I didn't know that. But it sounds like–"

Ms. Tober and the director, arguing with each other about the article on the panel, strode up beside him. The director appeared to be taking the issue personally.

"I don't know how something so inaccurate could be left up for so long!" he said, accusingly. "This article has been here for at least a week, Ms. Tober!"

"What is it?" Sam asked.

Director Nelson's eyes narrowed. "That's *not* the authorized text."

Hoping to prevent a diplomatic meltdown, Sam said, "Maybe it's a clue."

"What?" Ms. Tober asked.

Studying the written display, he began to warm to the idea. "The foam board that the information is printed on looks slightly different than the others," he said. "I mean, I don't have an artist's eye or anything, but–"

"But the fonts and right-hand justification is to a slightly different margin," Ms. Toben said. "Yes, I see your point."

The three of them stared at the board the text was printed on.

"What else?" Sam asked himself.

Ms. Toben cleared her throat and looked toward Nelson. "There *is* one other thing we spotted."

They led him to an exhibit on the first Soviet nuclear bomb, *First Lightning* or RDS-1. In the photographs, it was very similar in appearance to the *Fat Man* bomb the U.S. had created, except that the coloration was a solid gray.

There was a small smudge on the poster. Sam rubbed his finger over it, discovering what was left of a sticky patch from two-sided tape. Something that had been here was missing.

They led him over to the main display of the Chicago Pile-One and pointed out one of the figures. This one wore a baggy suit, commonly seen on Soviet scientists, and a Soviet flag.

"That's Andrei Sakharov," Ms. Toben said. "The chief engineer overseeing the Soviet nuclear design program at the time."

Sam ran his fingers over the display, discovering the tape mark where Werner Heisenberg had been fastened to the table—right next to Sakharov.

"Did the two men know each other?" Sam asked. "Sakharov and Heisenberg?"

"No, they never met," Ms. Toben assured him with the certainty of a well-read historian, no doubt holding a PhD.

Director Nelson cleared his throat. They both turned his way.

"I've heard -" He shook his head. "I've heard that Operation BIG buried more than a few secrets. We can't discount the possibility that the information we're finding here has some basis in truth."

"That's ridiculous!" Ms. Toben exclaimed.

"It wouldn't be the first time that we've uncovered history that shook us to the core," Nelson said gently. He reached out and patted Ms. Toben's trembling hand.

"But to threaten a nuclear explosion if that history wasn't revealed? What kind of psychopath could even do such a thing? Surely not a historian!"

"There, there," Nelson said, still patting her hand. He sounded as though he'd had experience with some less-than-sane military experts from time to time.

Sam shook his head. If he was following the insinuations that the terrorist was implying, then the German nuclear program was much further along than military historians had portrayed it. It seemed possible and seemed even likely that both the Soviets and the Americans had stolen far more research from the Germans than they had admitted.

Somehow Heisenberg was involved with both programs.

Had Heisenberg been a traitor to the Nazis? Had he acted in such a way to ensure that neither the U.S. nor the U.S.S.R. possessed a nuclear monopoly?

CHAPTER TWENTY-TWO

ON BOARD THE *MARIA HELENA*, CHESAPEAKE BAY.

TOM BOWER SCRATCHED his chin as he put down the phone.

Wasn't this one for the record? The man who'd called was supposedly the pilot of a Cessna Sam had used to fly into D.C. in order to face down the terrorist who was holding them all hostage with a World War II-era German bomb that shouldn't exist.

Sam Reilly, what have you gotten yourself into now? Everything's normal in our world.

The somewhat hysterical pilot told him a wild story — after calling to ensure his wife was okay, which she was. He had asked Tom to arrange a place for him to stay near the Capital Mall. Also, to help him find a way to keep the police from seizing his plane or arresting him for not filing a flight plan.

Tom had talked the guy off the ledge, so to speak. A few phone calls later, he'd arranged accommodation for the nervous airman during the lockdown, a makeshift hanger to temporarily store his plane, and a "get out of jail free" card from the Department of Defense.

Tom grinned. Not bad for a morning's work.

Meanwhile, the *Maria Helena*, the Deep Sea Expeditions ship he and Sam Reilly generally called home, had been moving into position. The vessel was now anchored off the Chesapeake Bay, near the mouth of the Potomac.

Sam was in D.C. and he made sure Tom knew it. Clearly, the terrorist had informed Sam that he wasn't allowed to communicate with anyone, or his friend would have phoned by now.

It was Tom's job to decide what to do about that.

Sam's phone had been recovered—or rather it had been delivered via courier to a Deep Sea Expeditions representative in Manhattan. No clue who had sent it. Elise was trying to track the delivery service back to the original client.

Tom didn't expect much from the search. Even a miracle-worker like Elise couldn't track someone with enough smarts not to leave digital footprints behind.

He walked into the room that Elise used as her onboard computer lab. "Find anything about that courier yet?"

The petite woman wore headphones and a sour expression on her open, strikingly attractive face.

"No," she said, sliding the headphone away from her ear.

"Anything about Goodson's past?"

"A few things. I do know that the guy doesn't fit the profile of a terrorist. A spy, maybe."

"How so?"

"Remember the KGB Spy Schools?" At his blank look she continued, "In the 1950's during the Cold War, the Russians used to immerse their spies into American life before they were sent to America to blend in. They had training camps with specially constructed towns mimicking American life. You know, Fords and Chevrolets parked in driveways with their windows down? Drive-in movie theaters, girls sipping milkshakes at their local diner while listening to the Beach Boys on the Jukebox? Does this sound familiar?"

"Oh, yeah. I guess so. Probably from a TV documentary I once watched."

"The guy reminds me of that. He claimed to be a German immigrant who arrived before 1946, but he doesn't have any supporting records before then—not that people back then would have known that. They would have had to go to a records office and pay a fee to look through that kind of stuff. Nobody's got that kind of time. He seems the kind of person who, without constant contact, you wouldn't notice the gaps in his story. Even then, you wouldn't guess his past."

"But now?"

"Now that kind of information is just a search query away."

"So, he was a spy?"

"I don't think so."

"No? The Germans sent him over here to bomb D.C., which means, he was definitely something."

"I believe he was a soldier, a German pilot—not a terrorist. Even the CIA didn't suspect him of being a spy. He would have contacted the Germans again after the war if he was covertly sending information. But there's no indication that he did."

"Okay," Tom said.

"I know that it's not the same thing as proof that he wasn't spying," Elise added, "But I can't find *any* signs of clandestine behavior or connection. All evidence suggests he was a grateful immigrant who just happened to be using a fake passport."

"Maybe he didn't like the Nazis?"

"He was willing to bomb for them, though."

"Sometimes people change their minds when they have to face real human beings instead of political propaganda. There's also another alternative."

Elise made a wry smile. "Which is?"

"Wilhelm Gutwein used his bombing run to escape Nazi Germany. His could be a fairytale defection story to even challenge Sean Connery in the Hunt for Red October."

She cocked an amused eyebrow. "You think Gutwein was

defecting?"

Tom shrugged. "It's a possibility."

"Then what happened to the bomb? If he relinquished it to the U.S. government, something like that couldn't have stayed hidden for very long, could it?"

"Actually, if he did hand the bomb over to the U.S. State Department, back in 1945, it's precisely the sort of thing that *would* remain permanently buried."

Elise leaned back, crossed her arms across her chest. "What are you saying?"

"What would the U.S. government have done if it was given a working nuclear bomb in January 1945?"

Elise shook her head. "That's nearly six months before the Manhattan Project successfully tested its first nuclear bomb at Alamogordo, New Mexico."

Tom swore. "You're saying Werner Heisenberg wasn't only responsible for the development of the first German nuclear weapon? He was also responsible for the nukes we dropped on Japan at the end of World War II?"

"Maybe. Maybe not." Elise's gaze swept the sky, following a procession of military helicopters as they flew overhead across Chesapeake Bay. She swallowed hard. "The real question is, if that's the case, then who would go to such lengths to reveal the truth about our history?"

"Perhaps they're not trying to reveal the truth at all," Tom said. "We can't rule out the possibility that someone's going to great lengths to make sure that the past remains buried."

"Or simply to make a buck on the deal?"

CHAPTER TWENTY-THREE

BENEATH THE CAPITOL, WASHINGTON, D.C.

Congressman Peter Grzonkowski stopped to catch his breath.

At the age of sixty-one he was the youngest of the three senators in the group, but right now he felt every one of those years. His heart pounded in his ears and every muscle in his body burned with exhaustion. He and the two other senators had been constantly moved since the attack on the capital had taken place. He felt like his little group was being driven like a herd of cattle as they raced deeper and deeper into the tunnel.

"Congress people, if you will keep following me, please?" The man in the dark suit from the security detail helped one of the older senators to stand. "We're almost there."

The three senators followed the CIA agent through the tunnel. Peter was at the lead, followed by Congresswoman Bledes, and Congressman Carmichael. A second black-suited agent followed behind. Pipes and wiring led them forward and down a long, curving tunnel that formed the labyrinth of secret passages and tunnels beneath the Capitol. Their journey had started under the Library of Congress, but the three senators no longer had any idea where they were.

The lead CIA agent walked quickly. The senators had to trot in their efforts to keep up.

After several long minutes, the lead agent led them to a set of steel stairs that rose into darkness.

"Where are we?" asked Congresswoman Bledes.

She received no response.

The five of them climbed the stairs, their footsteps echoing eerily back to them.

Finally, they reached the top, a steel door with a pair of bolts holding it shut and a small monitor mounted near the door. The agent checked the camera, then his earpiece. "It's clear."

The bolts snapped with ominous finality as they slid back in to the door, sounding like muffled gunshots.

The door opened. All three members of Congress put up an arm to block the bright sunlight shining on their faces.

The first agent pulled his dark sunglasses down and climbed out. "Wait here while I secure the area."

Peter watched the agent disappear.

Congresswoman Bledes turned to the remaining agent. "Where are you taking us?"

This time she received a response. "We're taking a short walk to the next set of tunnels, Congresswoman Bledes, where you will be met by other agents and escorted across the Beltway to safety."

"Thank God," she said. "And do we know who's responsible for this attack?"

"Not yet. But right now, every agency in America from the CIA through to every level of the military is working on it. No one can hide from that sort of concerted effort for very long."

Congressman Grzonkowski said, "We were informed there was a nuclear threat to the capital."

"Yes," came the agent's monosyllabic reply.

"How the hell did someone smuggle a nuclear weapon into

D.C.?"

"I don't know, Congressman." The agent stopped walking at the base of a ladder. "That's not my concern right now. My job is to get the three of you to safety, and that's what I intend to do."

"It shouldn't take long," the agent said, a comforting but vague comment. The three members of Congress visibly relaxed.

At the bottom of the steps, an agent, receiving information from the agent up ahead, said, "Understood. I'll tell him." He then turned and pointed at Congressman Grzonkowski. "You go first."

"No. Call me old fashioned, but I'd feel better if we got Congresswoman Bledes out of harm's way first."

The agent nodded. "That suits me fine. I've been instructed to protect all three of you."

Congresswoman Bledes smiled. "Congressman Grzonkowski, flattered by your chivalry though I am, we all know I'm nearly twenty years your senior and I have no more right than you or anyone else to survive. You go first. Besides, you will be quicker out across the open than I could hope to be."

Grzonkowski shook his head. "Not an offer, I insist. I wouldn't feel right. You go first. I'd like to see the five of us come out of this alive."

"Okay," Bledes conceded.

Congressman Peter Grzonkowski watched her climb the last couple steps and out into the opening above.

He followed a few seconds later until all five of them were out in the daylight and onto a residential street packed with cars and with people talking on their cell phones, pacing back and forth, arguing both softly and loudly. Children played basketball in the gaps between cars. Calm, quiet. Normal.

The members of Congress remained in a cluster. The two CIA agents seemed to melt into the pedestrians before and behind the senators, unseen but still present. Trees arched overhead. Townhouses lined both sides of the street.

A series of shots rang out.

Congresswoman Bledes gasped and fell back against her two male peers.

"She's been shot!" Peter shouted, as he held her up.

The crowd in the street scattered.

Ducking down, Peter asked, "Where did it come from?"

No one responded to him — or if they did, he couldn't hear it.

This time, everyone seemed to pick out the sound of the shot. A short cracking sound. Something you'd hardly notice, it was happening so far away.

This time, Peter dropped to the ground. He was there before he knew it. He didn't intend to fall. He'd been bending over Ms. Bledes when pain surged through him like an electric shock. He had been hit in the back.

Another distant crack.

The third Congressman fell.

The agents stood over the three Congresspersons calling for help in their earpieces.

Instinctively, Peter rolled over. The pain in his back stung, but it didn't feel like it was going to kill him. He met Carmichael's eye. The man nodded, like he would be okay, too. It was then he felt liquid on the grass beside him. Still lying on the ground, he ran his hand across his back and held it out in front of his eyes. His hand was covered in a wet, sticky, pink liquid.

"Paint?" he said, with incredulity. "Someone shot us with paint guns!"

Next to him, he heard one of the agents hurriedly speak into an earpiece. "The assets have been negated."

A pause.

"No, sir. Not dead. They used paint."

The three Congresspersons' sober, professional outfits were

all brightly decorated pink.

"We'll have to try to move out some other way," the agent said. Then, "All right. We're returning now."

Peter shuffled over to help Congresswoman Bledes up, but she didn't move.

He rolled her on her side. Blood flowed freely from her back. While he and Congressman Carmichael had been targeted with paintballs, her wounds were very real.

The agent came over to him and said, "We've gotta go! What's taking Congresswoman Bledes so long?"

Peter sighed heavily. "She's dead."

CHAPTER TWENTY-FOUR

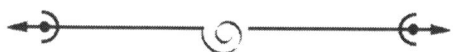

Ms. Zyla Needham walked through the locked archive. It was turning out to be a *very* long day. Ironically, the terrorist who had caused the city to be on lockdown was turning out to be the least of her worries. Several of her assistants had called in *"sick,"* a.k.a., unable to make it into the city via their usual commute.

Worse, the library was currently packed with worried tourists and commuters begging to know if they should stay in this building or demanding the location of the nearest bomb shelters. On top of that, a large number of Congressmen and women were making heavy research demands. It was all over the place. Everyone wanted to know everything about the nuclear program during and after World War II. *Where* was the proof of German bomb-making capability? Had anyone known that they had a bomb available to use against the United States?

In short, they were panicking.

She shook her head. Her phone buzzed, but she ignored it. She was on her break. Back in college while studying her Master of Library and Information Science, she had broken herself of the habit of smoking. Librarians who smoked were, in her opinion, an abomination. A librarian had no business bringing *smells* in among their precious documents. Ms. Zyla Needham had given up perfumes, scented lotion, and care products as well, but it was the lack of being able to step out for a smoke that got on her nerves.

Consequently, she treated herself with a walk through her favorite shelves.

When she turned the corner toward the Heisenberg Legacy, a man was already there. A dark suit and black sunglasses, his head turned slowly toward her.

She had a sudden urge to scream and run but suppressed it.

"Hello? Who are you? You don't have authorization to be here."

The man said, "My name's Smith. George Smith. I appear to be lost."

"Then allow me to escort you back to the public areas."

Afterward, she walked back to the shelves and checked the titles where he'd been standing. They were all smoothly set into place, nothing out of order, nothing different.

Still.

She pulled the binder case for the Heisenberg Legacy off the shelf. The other documents were valuable, too, but this one was personal for her, the great ethical question of her professional career.

She removed the case and opened the binder.

The document was still there. She started to close the binder, then stopped to look again.

And to read it.

Her eyes widened with horror.

She had read that letter literally hundreds of times during her years as a public servant. At the moment, whether that was wise or not wasn't the issue. The fact that she knew every word by heart was.

And the words written in print on the page had been changed.

She swallowed hard and burst back into the lobby where she had left Mr. George Smith, only moments ago.

He was, of course, gone.

CHAPTER TWENTY-FIVE

SAM'S NEW PHONE rang. "Hello?"

The disguised voice said, "The CIA just tried to smuggle three senators out of D.C. If they can't learn to follow directions, I'll hit the big red button and level D.C. Then it's *game over*."

"I'll let them know," Sam said drily.

"Good luck with getting the CIA to behave."

Ms. Toben screamed.

Sam turned to her, saw that she was watching a live news feed on the TV. The video was replaying a terrorist attack on a Congresswoman who had been shot dead while attempting to escape.

"What is it?" Sam asked.

"Congresswoman Bledes was shot and killed." Ms. Toben's face was ashen and her lower lip trembled. "We studied at college together. I've been friends with her for nearly forty years. She dedicated her whole life to making the lives of U.S. citizens better. This is terrible."

Into his cell phone, Sam said, "Are you happy?"

"She wasn't supposed to die," the garbled voice replied.

"But your men shot her!"

"That was someone else, not my men."

"Really?" Sam asked. "Are you saying your men didn't fire

at anyone?"

"They fired paintballs and most of the shots were intentionally aimed high."

"How do you know a stray bullet didn't ricochet and kill someone?"

"Because they were shooting blanks. That was the whole point. It was a warning. I hope they've learned from their mistakes. I told you that I would kill the next senator who attempted to leave the Capital. Next one who tries to escape won't be hit by a rogue sniper, they'll be struck by an intentional kill shot."

So, the guy didn't want to be a killer...

"How do we even know you have the bomb?" Sam snapped, letting anger come through his voice. "How do we even know it would've even worked? Our own military couldn't keep a World War II experimental German bomb up and running. What are *your* qualifications?"

He hoped that the man would snap back, giving away something.

Anything.

"You think I'm bluffing?" The words came out through a garbled robotic voice, but Sam was sure he still heard the amusement behind it.

"I think you're standing on top of a building with a paintball gun and a cell phone. And that's it. If you don't actually want to hurt anyone, what do you want to..."

"I didn't want to have to do this," the voice interrupted. "But you leave me no choice."

"Wait-"

Too late. The call cut off.

"What happened?" Ms. Toben asked.

"I don't know. The terrorist says he didn't shoot your friend."

"If he didn't, who did?"

"He doesn't know. Says there must be a rogue sniper out there acting alone." Sam swore under his breath. "There's something else, too."

"What?"

"He says, we have to pay the price."

CHAPTER TWENTY-SIX

THE EXPLOSION ROCKED the Smithsonian Institute.

Dust and small flakes of paint from the bomb casings displayed on the ceiling overhead fell. Sam took cover beneath a pile of sandbags used to depict a soldier's bomb shelter. Above, one of the large bombs swung dangerously in its wire harness.

Sam looked at the Director. "What happens if any of those bomb casings overhead fall?"

"Obviously, no explosive material is within those bombs," the Director said. "Although I wouldn't stand directly underneath any of them."

Meanwhile, Ms. Toben's phone was ringing again. "Yes? No, we're safe. What?"

She put her hand over the mouthpiece and turned to Director Nelson. "A number of explosions have occurred across D.C., Director."

"Oh, my God. Is anyone hurt?"

"They don't know yet."

Sam was shaken. He'd underestimated the terrorist.

The phone rang again.

"Yes?"

"Do I have your attention now?"

"You do."

"Good. Now, as I previously stated, I don't *want* to have to hurt anyone, but I will if I have to."

"Understood."

"Now, tell me. What have you found?"

Sam stood up and climbed out of the mock-bunker. His eyes swept the ceiling where everything appeared to have settled into place. He looked around, back toward the display where they found the figurine of Werner Heisenberg and Andrei Sakharov.

"I don't know yet," Sam admitted. "I'm still trying to make sense of it."

"Don't tell me you've lost the game already?" the garbled voice replied. "I thought you'd be better than this. Should I just press the little red button now and be done with it?"

"No, no! Wait!" Sam shouted. "We've found two figurines that don't belong in the Atomic Age exhibition."

"Go on."

"Werner Heisenberg and Andrei Sakharov."

"Good, and do you know your history?"

"Werner Heisenberg won a Nobel prize for his theory of quantum mechanics, which later proved to be the ground work to the development of nuclear fission and the atomic bomb. During the second World War, Heisenberg became the principal scientist for *Uranprojekt*—the German Nuclear Weapons Project."

"And Andrei Sakharov?"

"He was the leading Soviet physicist and designer of the Soviet Union's RDS-37, a codename for their thermonuclear weapons development program. Interestingly enough, he was also an activist for disarmament, peace, and human rights. His efforts toward civil rights reform led him to state persecution and later earned him a Nobel Peace Prize in 1975."

"Excellent work. They said you were meant to be bright. Maybe they weren't so wrong after all."

"Now what?" Sam asked.

"Work out what the two men really have in common and what you know about history might start to unravel."

Sam said, "They both worked on their respective country's first development of a nuclear weapon."

"Sure. Everyone knows that. The history books even agree with you. Find out what isn't published—what has been intentionally concealed for many years—and we just get ahead in this game. Until then, you're no better to me than anyone else."

Sam felt his heart race. "Okay."

"Okay, what?"

"Okay, I'll work it out."

"Good. To show that I'm taking note of your effort with the first task, I've left you a reward."

"A reward?"

"There's a car parked in front of 1530 Bleaker Street, a 1979 Buick LeSabre, dark green. I haven't left you the keys—you're not going to want to drive it yourself. The material in the trunk should be shielded well enough, but you never know."

"Understood."

CHAPTER TWENTY-SEVEN

THE DIRECTOR AND Ms. Toben were starting to exchange startled looks. Sam followed their gaze over to one of the printed signs.

Sam looked away. Now was not the time to be distracted. "And then what?" he asked his mystery caller.

"Haven't you found the next clue yet?"

Sam didn't answer.

"Be there in twenty minutes. Or it's game over, man. Game over." The terrorist gave an evil chuckle. When heard through the radio garbling device being used, it came out like a malevolent cartoon character.

Click.

Sam lowered the cell phone from his ear. If this guy expected him to be in place in twenty minutes or less, then it was close, wherever it was. Somewhere on or near the Mall.

He quickly took the Director aside and told him about the car parked on Bleaker Street, admitting his own guess about what it contained.

"Mr. Reilly!"

Sam turned toward the other two. Ms. Toben was pointing excitedly at writing on another panel.

"What is it?" he asked.

Ms. Toben began reading the text out loud. "The first nuclear device was detonated on July 16, 1945, in the Jornada del Muerto desert of New Mexico. It was code named JX234.A23 81st, 1st 1949 L," she said triumphantly.

"I'm sorry, is that supposed to mean something to me?" Sam asked.

She smiled. "Of course! Its code name was, *Trinity!*"

"Another clue?" the director asked.

"It must be!"

"But to where, my dear, to where?"

Ms. Toben's finger stopped pointing at the text and began tapping her chin.

"Excuse me," Sam said. "You've both been helpful, but I'm going to have to run. I have new orders."

"Run? Where?" Ms. Toben asked, her eyes wide in alarm.

"That's some kind of document call number," Sam said. "And I seem to remember that there's a huge library near here. If one of you could point me toward the Library of Congress…"

Ms. Toben gasped.

Director Nelson grabbed Sam's shoulder, shoved him out the emergency exit, and pointed him down the sidewalk.

"Past the Capitol. Corner of First and Independence."

Sam took a deep breath.

"Wait!"

Ms. Toben shoved a slip of paper with the code into his hand.

And he was off.

CHAPTER TWENTY-EIGHT

SAM SHOVED HIS way through the bystanders on the sidewalk. There were more of them than had been here half an hour ago. The tour buses and cars parked on the road had been turned off and everyone was standing around.

A man in a white shirt grabbed Sam's arm as he ran by. Sam jerked out of his grasp.

"Stop him! He's one of the terrorists!"

Sam cursed the man's stupidity and kept running. A pair of big men in front of him on the sidewalk crossed their arms and strode toward him. Sam dodged between a pair of tour buses, hopped on top of a red car, banged his way rapidly across the roof, then leaped onto a black SUV.

At the end of the parked cars, he jumped down and onto the grass of the Mall.

Sam's heart raced with anxiety. He heard a squirrel chittering angrily as rows of trees flashed by.

"Stop him!" The shout was further back now.

A group of people in front of Sam gaped at him, mouths open.

"What's wrong?"

"The terrorist's back there!" he yelled, pointing toward the men on his trail.

A couple of screams came from behind him as he kept running.

He crossed a street. The American Indian Museum was on his right, a rippling building that looked like it was being viewed from under a stream.

He was far enough away from his pursuers now, that their shouting had faded into the general noise of the busy public areas.

Looking both ways, and behind him, he crossed another street. Suddenly the Mall opened up onto the reflecting pool in front of the Capitol building. All it was reflecting at the moment was blue sky.

The street alongside the pool was more heavily packed with loose pedestrians, some of them sitting on their hoods. The sidewalks were jammed with strollers, bikes, little kids crying.

The Botanic Garden to his right looked relatively clear.

The wrought-iron fence wasn't hard to climb. He was over in about five seconds, ducking through a pair of trees, over a rock, and pounding down the trail.

Gravel crunched under his feet.

He jumped a hedge, danced over a brick half-wall, splashed through a shallow fountain, ignored a group of old ladies with red hats and jumped over another hedge.

Then he bolted past a big marble building surrounded by a formal English garden, and out the other side.

The Capitol building was off to his left, now.

His skin crawled. He felt himself being watched.

The terrorist? Or just over-eager security forces working their shift at one of the most important buildings in the country?

Had to be both.

Even the trapped tourists weren't brave enough to get too close. Sam tore down the grass, hell bent for leather.

His feet thudded on the street as he crossed. The Capitol was now behind him.

In front of him was the big white marble building of the

Library of Congress. Holy smokes! There were more stairs here than Rocky Balboa would want to see on a daily basis. Tarnished bronze statues. Long columns reminiscent of ancient Greece.

He headed for the main doors.

A piercing whistle echoed from the building.

"Sam Reilly!"

A figure stood at a side door near the street, waving what appeared to be a white flag.

Correction, waving a white cardigan.

Sam changed direction, dodged a wild-eyed man driving a golf cart filled with plants, and arrived at the side of a slender woman putting her sweater back on. Half-rimmed glasses hung around her neck on a chain, but she couldn't have been older than thirty. Her hair was pulled back with a pencil in the bun.

She looked pale and shaken, as if the terrorist attack were hitting her particularly hard.

"Sam Reilly?"

"Ma'am." He was panting.

She smiled, looking exhausted but showing dimples. "Follow me. The Director of the Air and Space Museum says you need help finding a book."

"Yes, ma'am. And fast."

"It's Miss," she said. "Ms. Zyla Needham. Inside, please. We're retrieving the document as we speak."

CHAPTER TWENTY-NINE

Sam was led to a small room with a table, chair, and a computer. "Coffee?"

"Just the document," he said. "What is it?"

In a strained voice, Zyla said, "It's the North Atlantic Treaty. The actual, original treaty. As you can imagine, we can't exactly let you walk out of the library with it. It's irreplaceable."

"Then shouldn't I be wearing white cotton gloves or something?"

"If you like."

The two of them waited. Sam checked the phone.

No new messages. He'd made it to the library on time. With growing trepidation, his eyes focused on his watch, he saw it tick past the twenty-minute mark.

Without meaning to, he held his breath.

The last time he'd made an assumption about the terrorist…

He waited for an explosion but either there wasn't one or the sound was unable to penetrate the thick walls of the Library of Congress.

A breathless library aide appeared with a slim blue leather-bound document in hand. "Here it is, Ms. Needham. Uh, and as far as anyone can tell, no sign of him anywhere."

Zyla shook her head slightly. *Not now.*

"Thank you, Troy." She accepted the document, laying it

almost reverently on the table in front of Sam. "A piece of history."

The leather had a small plastic sleeve attached with the call number coded on it. When he opened the front cover, a slip of onionskin paper identified the document as the original agreement of the North Atlantic Treaty. It was dated the fourth of April, 1947.

Sam wasn't a historian. He cleared his throat.

"Yes? It's the right one, surely, or at least the one that Director Nelson instructed us to bring to you."

Sam checked the code against the sweaty piece of paper he'd shoved into his pocket.

The codes matched up, all right.

He licked his lips.

"Ms. Needham," he said, "either this is a typo, or we have a problem."

She glanced at it, then did a double-take.

"That says 1947. But the call number lists 1949 as the year of publication."

He nodded. Zyla reached in front of him and turned the sheet of onionskin. Sam was no expert, but the linen paper of the pages of the treaty seemed authentic.

But the date 1947 appeared on several pages.

They reached the signature pages.

"Wait."

Sam made Zyla flip back to the first of the signature pages, then started counting.

"What is it?"

"Thirteen signatures."

"Thirteen…?"

"I only noticed the number was off because of one of them," he shifted through the document, "this one."

He pointed toward a large, looping pair of signatures under the words, "FOR THE UNION OF SOVIET SOCIALIST REPUBLICS / POUR LA UNION DES RÉPUBLIQUES SOCIALIISTES SOVIÉTIQUES."

"I'm no historian, but I know that the U.S.S.R. wasn't part of NATO in the Forties," Sam said.

The librarian hissed between her teeth. Her face was turning red with rage.

"It's a fake. *Another fake.*"

CHAPTER THIRTY

Shaken, Zyla turned toward the door, where her aide Troy awaited further instructions. His face was pale, too. He'd pulled his phone out and was jabbing the screen with a shaky hand.

"Another fake?" Sam asked.

"I discovered another document that was replaced, the text changed."

"What was it?"

She shook her head. "It has nothing to do with this. We're going to have to go over every document in the library to verify them and put still more security features in place. It's like we can't trust anything anymore." She took a breath. "Let's focus on the issue at hand. Troy, who knows anything about post–World War II politics? We need someone ASAP."

"I know some of it," Troy said.

"Talk," Zyla ordered.

He puffed out his cheeks. "Mr. Reilly's correct. The treaty was signed in 1949, not 1947. In 1955, the Soviets and their allies set up a rival treaty organization under the Warsaw Pact. The USSR certainly didn't sign NATO."

"And?"

"NATO was supposed to protect Europe from the Soviet bloc countries during a nuclear attack or a Soviet invasion. How that was supposed to work, nobody really knew, and the organization didn't mean squat until the start of the Korean War in 1950. In fact, even after that, NATO was considered to be so weak a deterrent that the French withdrew in 1966 and started setting up their own nuclear deterrent program. After the Berlin Wall fell, former Soviet bloc countries started drifting out of the Warsaw Pact and into NATO, one after the other."

He shook his head. "I only know that much because my Uncle Matt was a captain in the Army in the Nineties, and he had to go over to Bosnia in 1993 as part of a NATO-directed joint force. He met his wife there, and then of course NATO was invoked after 9–11 when we deployed joint troops to Afghanistan."

"So why would we be directed to a fake copy?" Sam mused.

"And where's the original?" Zyla asked in a strangled voice. "Where are all the originals?"

Compared to the potential death of a million people, it seemed as though the librarian had a few issues with her priorities. Then again, she might not know the stakes.

Sam flipped back to the first page of the treaty. "Only one way to find out."

CHAPTER THIRTY-ONE

PENTAGON, VIRGINIA

"M̲ADAM SECRETARY," TOM said, as he entered her office. Her nostrils flared. "Tom! What are you doing here?"

"Sam sent for me. Don't worry, he didn't put anyone at risk. I was able to work my way in without being seen."

"Tom Bower, do you know how many lives are at stake? We've just had undeniable evidence that the terrorist has the bomb, and that the bomb is still live."

"What evidence?"

"You'll be interested to know that the terrorist left Sam a plutonium rod in the trunk of a parked car near here."

"What a wonderful gift," Tom said, cheerfully.

"And before you ask, no, that's not enough to render the bomb inoperable."

"Shame."

"Since you're not with Sam, I'll assume that you have something you need to tell me in private."

"I do. Elise has been looking into William Goodson's, a.k.a. Wilhelm Gutwein's, past."

"And?"

"We got it all wrong!" Tom said emphatically, knocking his

knuckles on the desk.

The secretary took a deep breath. "Tom, so help me…"

He chuckled. "All right, I'll stop torturing you. Gutwein wasn't a Nazi."

"What? But he was ordered to drop an experimental nuclear bomb on Washington, D.C.!"

"Membership within the National Socialist Party—which wasn't actually socialist, by the way—wasn't quite obligatory at the time. Highly encouraged, yes, but not required."

The secretary waved her hand. "Go on."

"Gutwein had a number of German Jewish friends before and during the war. Elise was actually able to track down a few records of survivors who had later spoken of their friend and even looked for him after the war to thank him. But by then Gutwein had disappeared, with William Goodson in his place. They assumed he was dead."

"So why did he try to drop the bomb on D.C. in the first place?"

"He didn't," Tom said. "I've had a look at the historical and current maps of the area where the bomb was found."

"And?"

"And it's to the northeast of D.C."

"So?"

"So, he must have flown around D.C. to get there."

Her mouth dropped open for a second, then closed tight.

"I think he intentionally found an unpopulated place where he could safely put the plane down."

"Why?" she asked.

"Because Wilhelm Gutwein was trying to defect."

She raised an incredulous eyebrow. "To intentionally abdicate the power of God over his fellow men. *Why?*"

"Maybe he wanted out," Tom said. "He couldn't stand the Nazis anymore, he wasn't married and didn't have a family.

They'd been killed—"

"—In a previous Allied bombing run!" the secretary exclaimed, finishing his sentence. "It doesn't make sense! The man crash-lands a plane carrying a nuclear bomb, then hatches an elaborate plan to be carried out nearly eighty years later in order to take his revenge on the city that he avoided destroying in the first place? No. He was blown off course and landed where he *had* to."

Her face had turned red and angry. He'd be lucky if she listened to a single word he said.

The Secretary of Defense had known Tom since childhood, but he'd known her for that long, too.

She'd listen. He'd make her.

He took a deep breath. "Madam Secretary, what if we were wrong?"

"Wrong? About what, now?" she asked sarcastically.

"Wrong about what's happening."

"How?"

Her voice was still angry, but at least she was listening.

"We assumed that he wasn't actually happy to be here. That he only had the appearance of a grateful immigrant, doing what he loved—flying. He married. Had a son. Saved his money for a rainy day."

The secretary snorted. "And secretly transferred his enormous Swiss bank accounts to his new identity."

"Yes. But even those he didn't touch. He saved it all up for a rainy day. And we assumed that it was all so he could have the bomb dragged to somewhere in D.C. so he could torture us for a few hours, make us dance to his will, then destroy us."

"Yes, exactly. He wasn't saving for a rainy day, but for a thunderstorm filled with radioactive waste."

He ignored her interruptions. Her face was starting to soften with curiosity.

"The fact was, he was happy. It wasn't a facade."

"How can you say that? He's still trying to blow up Washington, D.C., and everyone in it."

"I don't think he is," Tom said. "And I don't think Sam thinks that, either."

"So the terrorist is playing this game in order to lead Sam to discover something? What? What could possibly justify–" She waved one hand toward the windows. "All of this?"

"I've no idea," Tom admitted. "I think Wilhelm Gutwein was persuaded to defect to the U.S. with the bomb, but someone betrayed him. Ever since then, he's been trying to put history right again."

CHAPTER THIRTY-TWO

SAM AND ZYLA spotted it at the same time. They looked up at each other.

"What?" Troy said. He was sitting on the opposite side of the table, trying to read the treaty upside down. "What is it?"

It wasn't a long document, in its original form, just fifteen articles.

One of which, Sam suspected, hadn't been in the original treaty.

It was currently numbered as Article 7, right after the article defining what constituted an armed attack on a member country.

Article 7 stated, *"All Parties hereby agree that all future developments of nuclear capability shall be shared with all other Parties, so that no Party may exclusively hold such power as to destroy the other Parties."*

"There's no way," Sam said.

"I agree. This must be another alteration."

"But why?"

"It seems to suggest that the U.S. and U.S.S.R. did share or should have shared their nuclear secrets with each other," Sam said. "Besides, the Soviets didn't explode their first atomic bomb RDS 1 — *First Lightning* — until August 29, 1949."

"I don't understand," Zyla said.

Troy spun the treaty around and read quickly. "Wow. Just… wow."

The change in angle seemed to show some kind of shadow on the page. Sam took the treaty back and examined the sheet in front of him. It seemed too regular to be an ink smudge.

He held the page up to the light.

"What are you…?"

"Troy," Sam said. "I want you to look up a phone number for me."

"Sure."

Sam read off a series of ten digits.

"I don't even have to look that up," Troy said. "I have *that* one memorized."

"What is it?"

"Old Tony's Pizza. It's on Pennsylvania and Third, a couple of blocks from here. I eat there all the time."

"How long has it been there?" Sam asked.

"Since 1979," Troy said without hesitating. "It's on the sign over the front door."

Sam gave Zyla another look, then handed her the treaty. Her lips went flat as she held it up to the light.

For a treaty signed in 1949 — or in 1947, for that matter — the phone-number-bearing watermark on the paper it was originally printed on was a lot more recent.

Sam took several photos of the document on the smartphone he'd been given. He then texted the images to Elise, with the question: *Please compare this with the original and see if you can make sense of what the terrorist is trying to show me.*

"What do you think any of this means?" Zyla asked.

"I've no idea, but I'm going to Old Tony's."

"For a pizza?" Zyla asked.

Sam shook his head. "No, for more answers."

CHAPTER THIRTY-THREE

*O*LD TONY'S HAD a sign over the front door stating that the place was established in 1979. It was one of those places that would have ordinarily had a line out the door. Today, it was almost empty.

Sam checked his phone, looking for a message stating that he had twenty minutes to find the next clue. If so, he wasn't going to make the deadline.

But there was nothing.

"Sam Reilly?"

A man in his fifties wearing a greasy apron came out of the alley along one side of the pizza place and waved to him.

Troy must have called ahead. Sam said, "That's me."

"Come this way. I have a booth saved for you."

"Thanks."

"I'm Tony, by the way." He wiped his hand on his apron and Sam shook hands with him.

"The owner?"

"Eh, now I am. The original *Old Tony* was my great-uncle. I've grown into the part, no?" He rubbed his gray-speckled chin stubble.

Sam chuckled. He was led through the busy kitchen to a back booth.

"It's just coming out of the oven," Tony promised.

"What is?"

"Your pie!"

Tony disappeared back through the kitchen door before Sam could ask another question.

He looked around. The place had dim lighting and smelled like pepperoni grease and yeast. The walls were dark green to match the front door sign. They were covered with old black-and-white photos.

The kitchen door burst open and Tony came out again, carrying a big white box, a tin plate, and a roll of silverware.

"No need to pay," he said as Sam reached for his wallet. "Your friend already took care of it for you."

"My friend?"

"Called about an hour ago. Paid and left a big tip. Enjoy!"

A note was taped to the top of the box.

FOR SAM REILLY — I THOUGHT YOU MIGHT BE GETTING HUNGRY. W.H.

W.H.? Who was W.H.?

Sam lifted the lid. A meat-lover's pizza with sausage, salami, pepperoni, ground beef, and Canadian bacon. It smelled delicious. He pulled off a slice, cheese stringing between the pie and his slice, and ate it steaming hot.

Tony brought him a Coke and a straw. "Good, yes?"

Sam nodded.

Sam leaned back. For a guy intent on destroying the city, he seemed to appreciate the place. And finding a terrorist thoughtful enough to order lunch — that stuck out, too.

Who was this guy?

A couple of slices later, Sam still didn't have a clue. He looked up. The photos in the frames above his booth showed a New York skyline, not one of D.C. That was odd, yet Sam was certain of it. There was no way that the body of water along the shoreline in some of the pictures was the Potomac.

In fact, he recognized the docks in one of the photos.

He'd been there before.

Unlike D.C., Sam had been around New York a fair amount, especially as a kid, accompanying his father back and forth from his various cargo ships.

Sam tossed the crust of pizza back into the box, wiped his hands on a napkin, and stood up.

Almost gingerly, he lifted one of the photographs from the wall.

In it, there was a boat floating along a dock, a big shipping boat. On the side was a name that Sam recognized.

Global One.

He turned the photo, tilting it back and forth.

Although Sam's division of his father's company was known as Deep Sea Expeditions, the overall holding company was officially Global Shipping, Inc. It had been founded by his grandfather. His very first ship had been optimistically called, *Global One.*

Standing in front of the boat were four people. In pen, someone had written the initials of each of them directly above the faces. He recognized the first of them. He had the initials M.R. and how could Sam not recognize him, the man was his very own grandfather, Michael Reilly. The second had the initials, A.S. and was Andrei Sakharov the Soviet scientist. The third person was shaking Andrei's hand, and had the initials W.H., just like the pizza.

Werner Heisenberg.

Sam studied the fourth person in the photograph. The initials were, C.F. He looked very young, with intelligent green eyes. Sam searched his memory for the face but came up blank. As far as he knew, he'd never seen the man before. That didn't matter, he had no doubt Elise would be able to put the image into a database and come back with a name.

He turned the photo over. On the opposite side was a

handwritten note.

It read:

> *I thought I'd remind you of this meeting. I hope you're all happy with the outcome. May God rest your souls, because I know my grandchildren never will.*

It was signed, *Wilhelm Gutwein.*

CHAPTER THIRTY-FOUR

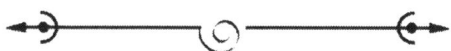

"Hey, Sam. You all right?" Tony asked. "You look like you've seen a ghost."

Sam turned to face him, still holding the photo.

"How long has this picture been here?"

"That one? Let me see. Ah! That's an old one. It's been here since the place opened. My great-uncle and grandfather immigrated here all the way back in the Forties," he said proudly. "This is one of the photos they took when they got here. They were shutterbugs, you know? Took pictures of everything."

"And who are these people standing in front of the boat?"

"Whatdya mean, people? There aren't no people."

Sam showed the photo to Tony. Now that he was taking a second look, he could see that the four of those in the photo had been clipped from another photo and pasted in."

Tony's face reddened. "What's going on here? What kind of moron pulls a stunt like that?"

Sam turned the photo over and looked at the back.

"Hey, what's that doing there?"

Tony reached over Sam's shoulder and snatched the piece of paper that had been tucked inside the frame.

"I don't even know what this means," Tony said. "What is this? Must be some joker of a college kid does something like that. Thoughtless is what it is."

"May I see it, please?" Sam asked.

Tony handed him the piece of paper.

Sam frowned at it. It was a code of some type.

"Can I have this?"

"You think that it's a message from your friend? He seems like the bad kind of a joker, you ask me. The kind of guy who superglues his best friend to a toilet seat."

"Oh yeah, he's a real joker, alright," Sam agreed wryly, taking a picture of the photo using his phone before returning it to the wall. "But do me a favor and leave it for a few days. The guy's not all right in the head. I wouldn't want to piss him off."

Tony gave him a sharp look. "You're working on the bomb case, aren't ya?"

"Good guess, but don't spread the word around. He's already thrown one fit that got innocent people killed."

CHAPTER THIRTY-FIVE

SAM CHECKED THE burner phone again as he stepped outside Old Tony's and onto the sidewalk.

Now what?

He couldn't call Elise or he'd piss off the terrorist. He couldn't miss his next "clue" or he'd piss off the terrorist. Damned if you do, damned if you don't.

He'd never heard any family history about his grandfather being somehow tied to Werner Heisenberg, let alone taking a photo with the famous scientist. Or Andrei Sakharov for that matter.

A taxi pulled up to the curb. The front passenger door popped open and a hand waved at Sam. "Call for a cab, mister?" a man with a broad east coast accent asked.

"Thanks!"

Uber had captured much of the D.C. taxi trade, but there were cabs available. Sam climbed into the seat, as happy as if the good fairy had granted him a wish. The moment he slammed the door, the cab pulled away from the curb.

Incredibly, traffic had cleared somewhat, so the car was able to move.

"Where you headed, mister?"

"To this place." Sam handed over the piece of paper.

The cabbie said, "Huh. I thought I knew every place in the

city, but sure as shootin' I don't know that one. Mind if I call my dispatcher?"

"Be my guest. I've no idea, either."

The cabbie dialed a number and read the code off to the person on the other end of the line.

"Take just a minute, mister. She's lookin' it up."

At the end of the block, the cabbie took a sharp right. The terrorist couldn't have opened up the Beltway. It must be the Secretary of Defense's work, getting people to clear the roads.

"Hey, whaddya know?" the cabbie asked. "Looks like she found it."

Sam breathed a sigh of relief.

"The World War II Memorial, Washington, D.C. It's gonna cost you, though," the cabbie warned. "It's north of the Capitol. Take us a while to get there, that is, as long as this traffic keeps moving."

"I don't mind," Sam told Tom Bower, not fooled for a moment by his fake accent. "If it gets too bad, I'll get out and walk."

"As long as you pay me first," Tom muttered. "By the way, mister, did you hear the news?"

"What news?"

"About the terrorist."

"Depends on how new the broadcast is."

Tom rapidly brought Sam up to speed about the continued lockdown, urgent government directives to house commuters and tourists around the city, and to start clearing the streets of their cars so emergency vehicles could keep moving and panicked parents could get their kids home from school.

He also told Sam about Congresswoman Bledes demise, and how the media reported that the rest of her party had been made secure in a bunker beneath Capitol.

Sam asked, "What about the death toll from the explosions?"

"There weren't any."

"Are you kidding me, the entire city shook!"

"Yeah, three buildings were leveled."

"Really, so why weren't there any lives lost?" Sam asked.

"All three buildings were set for demolition next week."

"Our terrorist simply sped up the process?"

Tom nodded. "It would appear so."

"Well that proves it."

"What?"

"Our terrorist doesn't want to hurt anyone."

"And then, if you can believe it," Tom said, "he decided to give proof that he had a nuclear bomb in the city."

"How?" Sam asked.

"He dropped off a plutonium rod. In the trunk of a car."

Sam's suspicion about the terrorist's cryptic message was confirmed.

"Was anyone hurt?"

"No. I heard it was sealed up pretty tight."

Sam's phone rang.

He and Tom looked at each other. Tom had been able to get into the city and find Sam–but the real test of whether they'd fooled the terrorist was now.

The disguised voice said, "You've found a friend, Sam Reilly."

Sam made a face, shaking his head at Tom. Tom pressed his lips together and started looking around them, trying to spot anyone watching.

Sam was tempted to make a smartass remark, but the last time he'd let himself run at the mouth, it hadn't ended so well.

"That's three times you've pushed me."

Sam bit back another remark.

"You're not very good at playing by the rules, are you?"

If he didn't say something soon, the terrorist was going to blow up something else just to prove that he could still force Sam to play along. "Depends on what's at stake."

The terrorist chuckled.

Tom's phone rang.

"Tell your friend to answer that."

"Go ahead, Tom."

Tom's eyebrows lifted in the rearview mirror. He turned up the volume and answered, holding the phone across the top of the steering wheel. "Hey, Elise. What's up?"

"Tom. I've gone over the code you sent. The easiest, most obvious interpretation was that address that I gave you. But there's more."

"What is it?"

Elise paused, as if she had heard something odd in Tom's voice.

"The name of a ship that was scuttled off the coast of New York in 1996. The *Clarion Call*."

Sam frowned, but said nothing. Tom opened his mouth, but Sam raised a hand to cut off the logical question, shaking his head. He knew that ship.

Knew *of* it, at least.

He spoke into the burner phone. "We have your next clue."

The voice growled mechanically, "You had to cheat to do it."

"What else did you expect?"

"Get rid of your friend, Sam Reilly, or I will. I want him out of my city."

The call cut off.

Sam let out a breath. "The game's up, Tom. He knows you're here somehow. And he wants you gone. Drop me off here and I'll walk to the World War II Memorial. He says he'll let you leave the city—apparently, he doesn't want you getting in the way. He says he wants you out of his city. See if you can track down the location of where the *Clarion Call* was scuttled and start moving the *Maria Helena* in place. We're going to need to dive that wreck if we're ever going to find answers to this game."

CHAPTER THIRTY-SIX

THE *CLARION CALL* had been one of Global Shipping's earliest ships. Sam's grandfather, Michael Reilly, had bought it after *Global One* but before the firm had officially made its way out of the red and into the black.

At the time, the purchase had been considered risky. Not just because of the firm's finances, but because the ship had previously been owned by a Finnish black-market weapons trader, with ties to the U.S.S.R.

In other words, a smuggler's ship.

According to family legend, it was the first Reilly ship to have a secret compartment built into the hold. It wasn't used for smuggling arms or the secret human cargoes that had been rumored under the Finn, but works of art, antiquities, gold bars, and more.

Secrets.

Sam had his suspicions about his family's relationship to the U.S. government. He, himself, had assisted the Secretary of Defense on a number of projects, and he knew that the CIA was involved somehow.

The CIA was like a fungus. Once you let it in, it grew *everywhere.*

He had thought that it was James Reilly who had first entangled the family in such clandestine matters, but now that *Global One* and *Clarion Call* had been brought into this business, he was starting to reconsider.

What if their connections went back further?

Global One had been taken to a family property along the coast of Maine, dismantled, and scrapped. The fixtures from the captain's cabin had been moved into the house and recreated in a guest room. One of the smaller sea boats had been brought onto the grounds and turned into part of a children's playground. The name had been cut out of the side of the ship and hung in a place of honor over the fireplace.

But the *Clarion Call* had been scuttled. Sunk in deep water— 700 or more feet down, to be exact.

Gone without a trace.

As if it contained secrets that his grandfather had wanted to bury forever.

CHAPTER THIRTY-SEVEN

THE TAXI PULLED into the curb and Sam got out.

As Tom pulled away, Sam noticed the tug of additional weight in his left front pocket. He stopped to check the terrorist's burner phone. No new messages. He placed the phone back in his left pocket, noting the presence of a second phone.

Tom had taken a risk.

Sam approved.

In all likelihood, Sam's position and conversations were being picked up through the terrorist's burner phone. Tracked by GPS, the terrorist could have set it to transmit everything it picked up even when it appeared to be "off."

Sam had to get rid of the phone or block it. But how could he do that without the terrorist knowing he'd done so?

He couldn't even hand the phone off to a passer-by and offer them a twenty for walking the phone around the block while he made a few calls. The terrorist would hear.

Sam looked around. He was on a residential block lined with town houses. Single garages at the end of driveways, and old-growth trees. People sat on the front stairs and spoke to each other in low, worried voices.

A group of kids, enjoying the relative lack of traffic, played in the street. A trash can overflowed with paper bags and cups.

Flowerboxes sat on the tops of wrought-iron fences, blooming with blue and pink hydrangeas, red peonies, and gladiolus. The wind picked up, tossing a few leaves along the sidewalks.

Sam waited until the pair of kids got into a fight over a dog, then dropped the burner phone face-down in one of the flowerboxes. The black plastic faded almost invisibly into the dark soil.

He kept walking.

"Sam!" the Secretary of Defense exclaimed. "Where are you?"

"It doesn't matter, ma'am. I'm still in the D.C. area."

The secretary wasted half a minute explaining why it *did* matter, in her opinion. Sam grimaced. If she really wanted to know, she'd have to trace the call—by which time he intended to be elsewhere.

"I've spoken to Tom," he said.

"That idiot! He's putting us all at risk."

"Yes, ma'am." Sam neglected to mention that Tom had been caught out by the terrorist. "I've sent him back, as a matter of fact. We've received the next clue, and it leads to one of my family's old ships, the *Clarion Call*."

Sam knew that Tom would make a call of his own to the Secretary of Defense. His hope had been that he would be able to make one first.

It seemed to have paid off.

The secretary inhaled sharply, but said nothing.

"I've asked him to take the *Maria Helena* to the coordinates where the ship was scuttled. He needs to dive it. I think there may be further leads on that sunken wreck."

"I see," the secretary said.

She was far too experienced to blurt out what was on her mind, but she couldn't conceal the fact that there *was* something significant about the location.

"Ma'am," Sam said. "I've found three different 'clues' on this treasure hunt so far. Let me tell you about them. I have less than ten minutes before I have to cut off this call and power down the phone."

"Tell me then, and quickly."

He gave her the rundown of the information he'd learned at the Air and Space Museum, the Library of Congress, and *Old Tony's* — the picture of *Global One,* and the four men in front of it.

"What conclusions did you draw from these mysterious tip-offs?" the secretary asked, when he was done.

Her voice sounded stiff. What he had told her had affected her somehow.

She knew more than she was saying.

"That this has something to do not just with the Germans during World War II, ma'am, but with the Russians as well. There's something else you should also know."

"Go on?"

"My family was involved."

"It seems that way. What else?"

"I couldn't say."

"You don't know, or you couldn't say?"

"There's a question I wouldn't mind asking *you.*"

She snorted, but said nothing.

Sam added, "Let's just say that neither one of us is confident enough about our conclusions to talk about them openly. That way it doesn't sound like we're deliberately hiding things from each other."

The Secretary of Defense was an old friend of his family, but that didn't mean that Sam trusted her further than he could throw her.

The woman used to cheat at 'Old Maid' back in the day, after all, and later taught him how to double-deal and count cards so they could fleece his father at poker.

She was *definitely* not to be trusted.

CHAPTER THIRTY-EIGHT

THE NEXT CALL was to his father.

"Sam, is that you?"

"It's me."

His father paused, took a deep breath. "What's going on and how much is this going to cost me?" he asked.

Sam's father wasn't heartless, but he had a hell of a way of expressing himself. It was like living as a fish, while having a great white shark for a parent.

"You've seen the news," Sam said. "How much do you know?"

"I know enough to know that you shouldn't be on the damned phone with me."

"I've sent Tom out to dive the *Clarion Call*," Sam told him.

Which was strange in and of itself. If he wasn't supposed to have any help and he wasn't supposed to go beyond the Beltway—how in the world was he supposed to follow a clue? The terrorist must have known that he'd find a way to cheat at that point.

He must have been counting on it.

Sam grimaced.

"The *Clarion Call*," Sam's father said. "That's one of our oldest vessels. Sunk off the coast of Sandy Point State Park. Before my time. It was one of old man Reilly's ships."

Sam waited.

"I'd always wondered why he scuttled it," James acknowledged. "It was supposed to have been in poor repair, but I'd been on it a few months before that, and it didn't seem in disrepair. Nothing that couldn't have been repaired, anyway."

"It was the first of the 'special' ships, wasn't it?"

James chuckled. "You might say that."

"So there might have been something hidden inside?" Sam asked.

"It sounds like exactly the sort of thing my father would have done. He would've taken on the job to hide something, accepted payment for the job, then taken the cost of the sunken ship he'd just been paid for off his taxes. He was a hard man, old man Reilly."

In that case, pot, meet kettle. Like father like son.

"What might be in there?" Sam persisted.

"Anything. It went down in 1996. By then he had contacts all over the world."

"Something illegal?"

"Probably."

"How illegal?"

His father paused. Finally, he said, "He never smuggled women, as far as I know."

"Dad…"

"It's a long story. And you don't have time."

"What about *Global One*?"

"What about it?"

Sam explained about the picture and his theory that it all had something to do with the Russians.

His father made a thoughtful humming sound in the back of his throat. "I don't know what to say, Sam. I do know that the *Clarion Call* was used to ship something from Canada to Russia, back when it was still the Union of Soviet Socialist Republics."

"How is that connected?"

"I remember the cigars they used to smoke. The three of them would stand on the deck and smoke them after supper, with the full moon overhead…"

"The three of them?"

"I don't remember much. I was young. Mama was always sick on the water, even on the big ships. 'The boy has to know where he came from,' Dad would say, and drag me across the ocean without her, but then he'd abandon me. Stan and I used to bet on horseraces, listening to the results over the radio all night long."

James Reilly wasn't one to share stories out of the past, and he wasn't one to let his mind wander. If he did, he had a good reason.

Sam waited, hoping that his father's memory would bring up whatever was swimming around in the depths of his highly intelligent mind.

James said, "Nothing good. That's all I remember."

"Another question. Did Grandpa ever meet Werner Heisenberg?"

"The scientist? No."

Sam set his jaw hard. Oh, well. He hadn't exactly expected to hit gold with the first strike of the hammer. "Look, dad. Will you see what else you can find?"

"Call you back at this number?"

"Yes."

His father grunted, said, "Don't do anything that hurts our stock prices!"

On the way back around the block, Sam picked up the phone and checked it.

So far, so good. No angry messages, no sounds of explosions, and no voice mails from the terrorist stating that he had pushed his luck too far.

That was good.

He was planning to push it even further.

CHAPTER THIRTY-NINE

THE RESIDENCES AT FARRAGUT, WASHINGTON, D.C.

Retired Senator Charles Finney sat in his wheelchair on his balcony at The Residences at Farragut. He was still sore from his morning's efforts. It was a nursing home, plain and simple, although the staff didn't let any of their patients call it that. The place was so expensive it felt more like being on a permanent pleasure cruise than anything else, but so restricted, it reminded him of a top-security military base, too.

He could have ordered lobster for breakfast if he wanted—but he couldn't have walked out of the building of his own free will, even if he could still walk.

His balcony overlooked Farragut Park—he could just see the back of the White House from his floor. He'd picked the apartment based on the view alone.

Charles Finney wanted to remind himself of who he was, a man who'd lived his life in the shadow of that great building, a man who'd made sacrifices for his country.

If anyone found out what he'd done, it wouldn't just be his own image that was tarnished. It would destroy the entire fabric of democracy, and what this great nation was founded upon.

He shook his head and cursed.

The terrorist seemed to be intent on destroying everything

he'd built. He'd unearthed *Die Koloratursoubrette,* the bomb that Heisenberg had jokingly named "The Fat Lady" of opera, after he had heard that the American bombs were to be named "Fat Man" and "Little Boy."

Then he'd dragged Mike Reilly's grandson into the situation, leading him around by the nose from clue to clue. At least, that's what he was hearing from his sources at the Capital.

It was a bad sign.

He'd had to take steps. The death of Congresswoman Bledes was unfortunate, but Finney considered her loss collateral damage. He was mostly indifferent to her death. What stirred his anger was the fact that the shot had failed to reach its intended target.

What else would be lost to protect the king in this game?

He chuckled to himself. He'd given up so much, in a thousand small ways; he wouldn't hesitate to sacrifice himself now—except for the fact that he had to play both the role of a piece and of the player.

It was worth it, though.

The King was the United States.

And he'd be damned if he was going to yield the game to the son of some upstart German immigrant trash…

Finney wheeled himself back inside, and away from the balcony. He was humming an old Doris Day song in the back of his throat.

A knock at the door.

"Come in."

A pretty, pale-faced young woman stepped in. "Someone here to see you, Mr. Finney."

"That's all right. I'm expecting him."

She backed out of the doorway; a few moments later, George Smith entered. He had an aluminum attaché case with him, attached to his wrist by a discreet cuff and a black band that looked like a bicycle lock.

"Sir," he said.

"Do you have it?"

"Yes, sir. We used the paintball attack on the senators as a distraction. As you guessed, the terrorist had to respond to the attempted escape you asked us to put into effect. I believe we timed things rather well."

"Yes," Finney nodded in satisfaction. He knew the document had been held in the Library of Congress. Several of his people were planted there.

"Would you like to see it, sir?"

He rubbed his tongue thoughtfully over a tender tooth. He had lost a few over the years, and he hesitated every time he had to have one pulled.

"Might as well," he said. "Before it goes into the secret vaults, eh? We're turning into the Vatican, with underground crypts full of history. Crucial information it's better that no one knows, yet we can't bear to part with. A bunch of sentimental old fools, that's what we are, too ashamed to admit that we're a bunch of filthy sausage-makers. Each and every one of us push it down the road, make it someone else's problem..."

Smith stood and listened with his hands behind his back. Respectful treatment toward a key political figure who had once been important, but was now just an old man who was clearly losing his marbles.

He shook his head. "Listen to me ramble. Go on, open it."

Smith unlocked the case from his wrist, then placed the case on the bedside table and unlocked the two clasps with a key. He snapped open the locks, then lifted the lid and pulled out a manila envelope. Inside the envelope was a rigid plastic folder.

Inside the folder was the document, still inside a thin layer of crisp cellophane.

The old man's eyes filled with tears.

His sadness wasn't for the author of the letter—Werner

Heisenberg—or the addressee—President Gerald Ford—but for all the times gone past. The burdens he carried, the lies he was forced to tell, even the deaths he had to order.

All to protect D.C. from one bomb. A device that had been ripped out of the past where it had been decently hidden, then placed in public view.

A million people, threatened.

It made his blood boil.

And for what? So that some kid could reveal the "truth." The one truth out of a hundred different other truths that nobody needed to know—nobody needed to know that the Germans had been ahead of both the U.S. and the Soviets. Nobody needed to know that World War II had almost been lost. If Washington D.C. had been taken out by a nuclear bomb, would all the fight have gone out of Americans? If anyone found out how close the U.S. seat of government had come to becoming another Nagasaki or Hiroshima, who knows what would have happened.

Most importantly, few people would accept what he had withheld for more than seven decades: In the history of the human race, no one event had steered the course of humanity toward everlasting peace, more than the development and subsequent proliferation of the atomic bomb.

In his opinion, J. Robert Oppenheimer, the lead scientist who worked on the Manhattan Project, and subsequent architect of the first proven successful atomic weapon, should have been awarded the greatest Nobel Peace Prize for his development.

It was this action and the deterrent threat of life-on-earth ending consequences, that left the world in its longest period of peace and stability since the end of World War II. At no time on earth had mankind cooperated so well together, since the start of the Agricultural Revolution nearly ten thousand years ago.

Retired Senator Finney closed his eyes.

A group of scientists brought this atrocity to mankind. And

in jarring contrast its development had left prolonged peace.

But it was his own actions which brought about the proliferation of the world-ending weapon. This was what made the entire venture so successful.

If America had maintained the Atomic weapon monopoly, the benefits would have been nowhere near as successful. In that case, he doubted the city of Nagasaki would have been the last place on earth to be destroyed by such a weapon.

The thought literally made him shiver.

What they did was abhorrent and treasonous at best, but he had done so for the good of his country. He was old. There was nothing the Administration could do to him that time wasn't already well on its way to achieving.

What use to drag it all out into public now?

Except to blackmail the good men who were forced to make such terrible choices.

He shook his head and dashed the wetness in his eyes away with the back of his hand.

"Hand me my reading glasses," he said.

They were gently placed into his hand.

Finney read the document letter, the words swimming in front of his eyes.

Although it seemed to take an eternity, he soon finished reading. His mouth was dry as he swallowed. Smith handed him a glass of water as he took away the document.

"Sir?"

"Lock it back up."

Heisenberg had been a man of probity and honor. The problem with men of probity and honor was that they were unable to keep their damned mouths shut. The letter had made President Gerald Ford ask questions. Questions, like earthworms, did their best work when they were buried deep underground with the rest of the muck. Ford's questions had exposed truths, forcing him to make difficult choices.

The Heisenberg Legacy was locked up again, the band and cuff discreetly out of sight around Smith's wrist. The man had worked for the CIA for several decades, if he remembered correctly.

"Sir?"

"All that fuss over a single piece of paper?"

"Yes, sir," Smith said, with some feeling.

"Well, be off with you. May you have a safe journey taking that to its new resting place."

"Yes, sir."

Suddenly, Smith held out his hand.

Bemused, the old man shook it. "What was that for?"

"I just want you to know that some of us know what you sacrificed, sir. You're respected for that."

The old man was touched. "I appreciate that, son."

Then the hand was withdrawn, the CIA agent gone, and the old man staring off toward the White House as it peeked through the trees off the edge of his balcony.

If only old Mike had still been around. He would have taken care of all of this with a snap of his fingers. Nobody had been harder than Mike…

Old Mike wouldn't have hesitated before ordering what *he* had dithered over for so long.

Finney picked up the telephone and dialed.

"Sir?" a man answered.

"There's nothing for it, Painter," he said, profoundly tired. "It's time for Phase Two."

"Yes, sir," said Painter, his voice somber.

Well, and why shouldn't he feel subdued?

Innocent people were going to die.

It was the price they had to pay to keep the world safe.

God knows, I paid the ultimate price to keep it secret.

CHAPTER FORTY

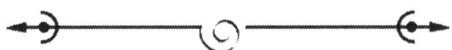

SAM KEPT MOVING at a quick pace along the now empty street, heading toward the memorial.

The bright sun shone overhead, pounding down into Sam's skull. He shaded his eyes and turned around in a circle. Everyone here had gone inside. The streets were strangely deserted, especially after they'd been so packed earlier. Both sides of the street were packed with cars, in some places double-parked.

There was a hush in the air. No music, no kids playing, no traffic.

Sam's throat tightened.

His grandfather had been a pilot in World War II. One of Sam's memories of the man was listening to him talk about the bombing of London. He said that first came the dual tone sound of the civil defense sirens. These were initiated by the Royal Observer Corps when they spotted Luftwaffe aircraft flying toward Britain.

This frightening sound caused civilians to stop whatever they were doing and rush into air raid shelters. Total blackout, everyone underground if possible—except for those brave souls waiting on top of buildings as spotters.

Suddenly, the sirens would cut off, and an eerie silence would come over the city. That utter soundless hush occurred—right before the bombs exploded.

The nightmarish contrast had stayed in Sam's mind.

That hush was what it felt like to Sam right now. A million innocent people, waiting to find out whether it was their day to die.

If he wasn't standing in the middle of the street witnessing this, he would have expected chaos. Streets full of panicked rioters, people on their cell phones screaming that they needed to get out of here *now* and to hell with everyone else. Horns honking, gas shortages, power out...

Instead, this eerie silence.

He had to fix this.

He had to stop letting the terrorist call the shots.

Given what he knew so far, he had two choices: track down this game-playing lunatic or track down the explosive device.

He was no bomb expert, but a bomb built in the 1940s shouldn't be that sophisticated–unless the terrorist had modified it. He should be able to figure out enough to dismantle any transmitting equipment, though, at least long enough to bring in a real bomb squad.

Then again, the Secretary of Defense, the Metropolitan police, the National Guard and many others likely had searching for the bomb covered. He might end up duplicating their efforts—and letting the terrorist escape.

If he were the terrorist, though, he wouldn't be *here,* in D.C. Why stick around to get vaporized by a nuclear fireball? No point.

But that led him back around in a circle. If he wasn't supposed to track down the bomb and this madman was somewhere else, what was he supposed to do then? Keep following the clues?

Continue to be led around by the nose?

The terrorist wanted him to know something about the Russians, the German nuclear bomb program, and—what?

First, he'd been sent to the National Air and Space Museum, to see altered evidence that the Germans had manufactured a bomb, called "Die Koloratursoubrette," at the Haigerloch Research Reactor during World War II, and that somehow Heisenberg and the Russian Andrei Sakharov had been involved.

Next, he'd been led to the Library of Congress, to see a fake copy of the North-Atlantic Treaty that had included Russia.

Finally, he was sent to the pizza joint, where he'd seen an old photo of *Global One,* where a group photo had been doctored in, including his grandfather, Heisenberg, and Andrei Sakharov, and a third person he couldn't locate.

Elise was still trying to work out the name of the fourth person in the photo.

He had no idea what Tom would find in the wreck of the *Clarion Call,* but the fact that it was on one of his grandfather's ships said something.

Start with the most obvious thing:

This all had to do with World War II.

Another obvious thing:

The Reilly family was unequivocally tied into this. Sam got the feeling that he was being blamed for the sins of his father, or grandfather, rather. But his impression of the old guy was that he had been harmless.

He rubbed both hands over his face, trying to think clearly. Sam knew he was confusing his memories of a sweet old grandfather with the real guy. Of course, old man Mike Reilly had treated his grandson with fond interest and care. But he was also a man who had founded a worldwide shipping company worth billions of dollars. "Ruthless" should probably be in Sam's description of him somewhere.

Important point: if holding Washington D.C. hostage was about World War II, that was before Mike Reilly had started up his shipping company.

Could this attack be concerned with something his grandfather did during World War II?

If he ever got the chance, he'd have to ask Elise to research who Mike Reilly had been involved with, and what he was doing during World War II. With luck, Tom might have already asked her to look into it.

Damn it. The mystery was eating at him. What was so important to the terrorist that he was willing to put a million people in danger? What could his grandfather have done that could possibly justify this to a terrorist's mind?

Even if Mike had flown a bombing run that wiped out the terrorist's hometown, it could never have totaled the equivalent of a *million* people. The Bombing of Dresden was estimated to kill 25,000 people. The bombing of Berlin, perhaps 50,000. Besides, his grandfather wasn't the only one involved in bombing Germany in WWII.

His grandfather wasn't responsible for hundreds of bombing raids.

Sam shook his head. It didn't make sense. Someone who just wanted the truth to be known from an old injustice didn't threaten innocents. Did a person burning for revenge lead people around on elaborate treasure hunts?

If this guy was ever found, he'd be one for the psychology books, no doubt.

Sam blew air out of his puffed cheeks. Either way, he was wasting time. Until he thought of something, the best thing was just to keep playing for time. Give the bomb squad time to criss-cross the city with Geiger counters. Give Tom time to find whatever was in the *Clarion Call*.

Sam headed up the stairs of the memorial site.

CHAPTER FORTY-ONE

WORLD WAR II MEMORIAL, WASHINGTON, D.C.

SAM WAS RUNNING out of time.

The monument was a pool, or rather a big fountain, with many smaller jets of water ringing the pool in the center, and a pair of larger water jets on either end. Here was something that hadn't been around long enough to have been built when Wilhelm Gutwein had first crashed his plane.

The memorial hadn't opened until 2004.

Fifty-six marble pillars and two triumphal arches surrounded the pool on either side. A wall covered by gold stars — each one representing a hundred American dead — ran along the back.

Sam had been here before, right after the opening. He'd been twenty-three at the time, and the place had been packed.

It was nearly abandoned now.

What am I looking for?

He already knew there weren't any specific mentions of his grandfather here, and none of Wilhelm Gutwein-slash-William Goodson. There simply were too many dead to memorialize individual names.

He was here. Now what?

He checked the phone again. He was over the time limit.

Turning in a slow circle, he waited for gunshots. Explosions.

Game over, man, game over, he recalled the words the terrorist had said to him.

But there was nothing.

Maybe something unforeseen had happened—something the terrorist hadn't planned.

Not the shooting of Congresswoman Bledes.

Something else.

Sam didn't know what else to do. He was in the middle of the World War II Memorial in D.C., and he was supposed to have found the next clue on this insane treasure hunt, but he hadn't.

He was coming up dry and he'd run out of time.

Any second, his phone would ring, and the terrorist would taunt him about the next clue. Might he even stoop to shooting another innocent?

Again, it didn't make sense. Paintball and a bullet? When he considered the Senator's death, it made him wonder if there might be another player in this game. A hidden figure on the board that no one knew was playing.

Sam's feet started leading him around the pool in the center of the memorial. The fountains provided a white noise like static that softened the sounds of the few other people in the area, turning their voices into hushed whispers.

The more time he had to think, the more he believed that the terrorist wasn't responsible for Congresswoman Bledes' death. One, the death occurred before time was up. It took time for news to spread, even on something like this. Two, he still didn't have a message from the terrorist.

Conclusion: her death had nothing to do with him.

Sam pulled out his phone.

He couldn't play by the rules anymore. He'd played by the rules—Congresswoman Bledes had died.

The terrorist wasn't in control of the situation.

He powered his phone on, pulled up the photo of *Global One*, and studied the one face he didn't recognize.

He thought about making some calls. His father, for one. The Secretary of Defense, for another.

But something was tugging at him. But what?

An old man in a wheelchair was being pushed around the memorial by a middle-aged woman. She fussed over him and said that they should just go back to the nursing home. He snorted and said that this was his afternoon out, and he'd be damned if he was going to let some subversive suicide bombing madman scare him away. Besides, if he was going to get blown off the face of the earth, he was going to say goodbye to some old friends first.

Sam couldn't suppress his grin.

The two of them abruptly turned off the main path toward a maintenance area, then stopped. The old man muttered something, and the woman chuckled, a reaction he took exception to. The man mumbled something else, the woman said something conciliatory. They rolled away to the north, the woman complaining about having to push him all the way past Farragut Park.

"Quit complaining," the old man said. "At least you have your damned legs."

In a few moments, they'd disappeared.

Sam stopped at the same place that they had, trying to work out what—aside from the obvious—had grabbed his attention. After a moment he spotted it. A cartoonish picture of a man hanging over the top of a wall, fingers and nose dangling, had been molded into the concrete of the wall.

Someone had been here. The terrorist?

On the ground beneath him was a piece of wadded up trash. Around it, some loose leaves were tumbling in the strong breeze.

Yet the paper didn't move.

Sam hopped over a short fence, walked down the ramp to the picture, and picked up the piece of trash. It had been taped to the ground.

He opened it. Another address, same handwriting as before.

122 K Street, NW. Washington, D.C

He dropped the address into the phone's GPS. It was within ten miles of *Die Koloratursoubrette*'s original crash location in Maryland. He started looking up the name of the owner in the public records.

The other phone, the burner phone, started to ring.

"You're still cheating, Sam Reilly," said the terrorist.

Sam's eyes narrowed. Even though the voice was still disguised, there was something subtly different about it. He waited to hear the rest of the terrorist's rant.

"I know you sent Tom Bower to the *Clarion Call* in your place - "

"Damned if you do and damned if you don't," Sam said. "You *wanted* me to send Tom out to that ship. You practically dared me."

The line went dead for a moment—it didn't drop out, thankfully. It went silent. Enough to make Sam literally start to sweat. Had he made another serious mistake?

Then the terrorist said, "You still broke the rules, Sam. You're going to be punished."

"Fine. Whatever you're about to do, you were going to do it anyway. Blow up all the innocents you want. You're the one in control here. Everything that happens here, from the death of Congresswoman Bledes to every other innocent who dies, that's on you."

Another long moment of silence.

Sam heard background noise on the line, and quickly added, "And you haven't even mentioned the fact that I've gone over my time limit without finding the next clue. What are you going to do about that? Or was this dead end planned all along, too?"

He was taking another terrible risk. But no matter what he chose, it was all a terrible risk.

Because that address was outside the Beltway. If he did what the terrorist wanted, the terrorist had an excuse to blow the place sky-high.

Yet if he didn't do what the terrorist wanted...

Who knew?

"But—" the terrorist said.

Then the line went quiet. Again.

As soon as the background noise came back on the line, Sam shouted, "What about Congresswoman Bledes? She was shot even before I got here! What about your damned rules now?"

He had his fingers crossed that the terrorist, operating outside the D.C. area, wouldn't have heard the news yet...

"Wait, what?" the terrorist said. "What?"

Then the line went quiet again, but this time it was suddenly cut off completely.

This wasn't just about a terrorist trying to destroy the American government, terrify American citizens, crash the stock market, and lead him around by the nose.

Sam had guessed correctly. Someone else was at work here, too.

Sam's cell phone started to ring again.

He answered it on the second ring. "Elise. Did you find anything from that photo?"

"Yeah, it belonged to a retired Senator from Virginia."

"What's the name?"

"Senator Charles Finney."

Sam let the name sit for a moment. It sounded familiar, but he couldn't quite place it anywhere. "Is he still in politics?"

"No. He has an exemplary record but retired several years ago after an accident left him in a wheelchair. Since then he's remained largely out of politics and all public life."

A wheelchair?

Sam shook his head. It couldn't possibly be the same guy, or could it? The terrorist wasn't omnipresent. If it was Finney, maybe he comes here every day at this time.

"Want to know the address of the rather luxurious retirement home he resides in?"

"Let me guess, 122 K Street, NW. Washington, D.C."

"Yeah, how did you know?"

"Lucky guess. All right. That's within walking distance of here."

"Then what?" she asked.

"Then I'm going to join Tom, and dive the *Clarion Call*."

CHAPTER FORTY-TWO

SAM KNOCKED ON the entrance door of the Farragut Residences. A receptionist greeted him, and let him in. She was an attractive lady in her early forties. Her combination of high heels and a slender dress that accentuated her figure made him think he was talking to a concierge at a fancy hotel more than an employee of a nursing home.

He explained who he needed to see and was given the room number.

"I'll ask if he's receiving visitors," she said, picking up her phone.

Sam nodded. "Okay."

She spoke quietly into her phone, hung up, and then said to Sam, "He will see you now."

"Thank you."

She smiled. "Do you know where you're going?"

"No idea."

"Take the elevator to the top. He's the only room on that floor."

"Thank you."

The receptionist took him all the way to the glass elevator, swiped her electronic keycard and then pressed the uppermost number. The elevator ascended the giant atrium all the way to the penthouse level.

Sam got out, knocked on a solid mahogany door, and waited. It had no number or name. Presumably, anyone who had access to the penthouse knew precisely who lived here.

The automated door opened inward.

An older man in a wheel chair met him. "Can I help you?"

Sam raised an eyebrow. "Senator Finney?"

"Retired," the man replied. "And you are?"

"Sam Reilly. I'm working on this terrorist attack."

Finney ran his eyes across Sam's disheveled appearance. "CIA or FBI?"

"Neither."

The old man smiled. "What are you doing here, then?"

"It's a long story," Sam said. "I'm following up a lead. If you want, contact the Secretary of Defense — she knows all about it. I'm told you remain in touch with a lot of people from Congress and the Pentagon and are familiar with her?"

Finney nodded.

Sam continued. "She'll vouch for me."

"It's all right, come in." Finney swung his wheelchair around, heading back into the main living area. "I don't have many State Secrets to protect and I sure as hell have the time."

Retired Senator Finney stopped at a large living room. It had floor to ceiling glass, overlooking a balcony with a view of the Capitol building, leading all the way through to the White House.

"Have a seat," Finney said, motioning to a three-seater leather couch. "You want a drink?"

Sam dropped into the comfortable couch. "No thanks, sir."

"All right, what's this about?"

Sam handed him the photo found at *Old Tony's* Pizzeria. "Do you recognize this photo?"

Finney took the photograph from Sam and stared at the image. "That's an old photo of now very old men."

"Sure is. Do you recognize any of them?"

"Can't say I do."

"Really?" Sam persisted. "I was told that's you, there, third on the right." He helpfully pointed. "It sure looks like you, doesn't it? I was hoping you might tell me who the other three men were and what you were all doing together?"

He took out his glasses and examined the photo more thoughtfully. "So it is."

"Now that you have your glasses, sir, do you think you could take a look at the other three gentlemen and see if their faces jog your memory?"

Finney slowly studied each face and frowned. "I'm afraid I don't."

"Nothing?" Sam asked. "But you were there."

"So you keep telling me, but I can't for the life of me remember it. You see, I was a very public figure. I had thousands of photos taken. How would I know?"

"Do you remember ever having a photo taken in front of the ship, *Global One?*"

"That name doesn't sound familiar, but I might have."

"Have you travelled on many large ships?"

"Hundreds, more's the pity. I was a Diplomat in the late 1940s. I spent a lot of time in my cabin, suffering seasickness. Terrible malady. Have you ever been seasick?"

"No," Sam said shortly. "Please, will you have one more look?"

Finney ran his eyes across Sam's concerned face and then dutifully studied the photo once more. This time he let out the softest of audible gasps. "Well. You're right, that photo indeed looks very similar to me. But it wasn't me."

Sam felt his heart race. "No. Who was it?"

"That's my brother."

"Your brother?" Sam asked. "I didn't realize you had a

brother. Do you know where I might find him now? It could be vitally important to cracking this case and neutralizing this terrorist threat."

Finney shook his head. "I'm afraid he went missing back in the late nineties and hasn't been seen since."

Sam said, "I'm sorry. Did you two have a falling out or something?"

"No. You misunderstand me Mr. Reilly. In 1996 my brother went out on a local fishing boat off the coast of Sandy Point State Park and never came back. They found his fishing boat capsized, but my brother's remains were never found."

"Again, I'm sorry."

"Yeah. Me too. My brother was a good man. But, that's life, isn't it? No one lives forever. He died doing what he loved."

"I suppose that's something." Sam stood up. "All right, I should go. I'm sorry to have taken up your time."

"Not a problem. I'm sorry I couldn't be of more assistance."

Sam glanced out the balcony, once more admiring the incredible vista from the Capitol building through to the White House. His smile was genuine. "You know, that's quite some view."

"Yeah, I bought the place so that I could wake up and look out at that view every day. It reminds me why good men — like you and I — work so hard for the betterment of our country."

Sam understood his patriotism. "Have you been following the terrorist attack?"

Finney nodded. "That's why we pay the price."

"What price?"

"Any burden we need to keep America safe."

"Congresswoman Bledes paid that price."

Finney cocked an eyebrow. "Congresswoman Bledes is dead?"

"Yes. She was shot while trying to escape the capital this

morning."

Finney paled. His hands twisted the rug covering his legs, looking flustered. "I'm sorry. I wasn't aware. Congresswoman Bledes was a remarkable woman. She alone has done more than most for this country." He paused, his gray eyes meeting Sam's. "What about her two companions?"

"Who?"

"I thought she was with Congressman Grzonkowski and Carmichael today."

Sam made a thin-lipped smile. For a retired Senator, he seemed well informed about the day to day itinerary of sitting members of Congress. "I'm sorry. I've no idea. I wasn't informed who she was with. But as far as I know, Congresswoman Bledes was the only fatality we've had so far throughout this entire terrorist attack."

Retired Senator Finney swung his wheel chair around toward the door. "You'd better get back to work Mr. Reilly. Someone needs to avenge her death, and you can't do it while you're in here."

"I'll try my best," Sam assured him, and walked out the door.

CHAPTER FORTY-THREE

Sam Reilly made his way along K street toward Franklin Square.

The boulevard was silent. Mercenaries or terrorists — whatever you wanted to call them — lined the southern side, mostly ignoring him, while U.S. marines and armored tanks lined the opposite end. It looked like something out of an urban warzone in the Middle East, not the U.S. Capital.

At the far end of the street a hot air blimp was tethered by a rope above a building, with a large advertisement for some local law firm.

Sam stared at the image.

His heart pounded in his chest as he felt that awful sense of déjà vu. He knew exactly where he'd witnessed that identical scene before. It was impossible, and yet almost certain. What was more unexpected was the fact he knew, with the same certainty, that he wasn't going to act on the knowledge, or inform the Secretary of Defense.

Not yet, anyway.

Sam still needed to complete his part in this evil game before it was over and he lost everything. He had to know what was hidden inside the scuttled wreck of the *Clarion Call*.

He kept walking east.

Sam unlocked his cell phone and dialed Elise's number.

She answered on the first ring. "How did your meeting go with retired Senator Charles Finney?"

Sam smiled, and kept walking. "We got it wrong. It was Senator Finney's brother, Joseph in the photograph."

"His brother?" Elise said, "I didn't find any record of a second Finney with matching facial features on the DMV for the past two decades."

"You wouldn't have. He disappeared, most likely dead, in 1996."

"The same year the *Clarion Call* was scuttled."

Sam swore. "Of course. Why didn't I think of that? It can't just be a coincidence. Everything keeps pointing back toward the scuttling of that ship—the *Clarion Call*."

"What do you want to do?" Elise asked.

"Has Tom located the wreck yet?"

"No, but the *Maria Helena's* not yet in position of the GPS coordinates your father gave him. Illegal or not, your grandfather kept records of the event."

"Really?" Sam asked. "That seems like a strange thing to do if you were going to try and bury secrets."

"The ship's in 720 feet of water. I suppose he was fairly confident the secrets would remain buried," Elise replied. "Besides, apparently the scuttling was all a big show."

"A big show?"

"Yeah. Someone out of the 832nd Ordnance Battalion US Marine Corps out of Fort Lee provided the ordnance required to sink the ship."

"Are you serious?"

"It gets better."

Sam said, "Go on."

"Who do you think was the officer in command during the scuttling blasts?"

"No idea. Who?"

"Major Roger Goodson. Alex's father!"

"You're kidding me! But Alex said he and his father had never really got along. Said he'd never learned why. His father was a military man—an Officer in the Marines to his core—while his grandfather opposed the military and had been a pacifist all his life."

"That might justify why Alex's grandfather and father never got along. They might both know the truth—whatever that is. One thing's for certain. There's something connecting the Goodsons with the Reillys."

"Thanks, Elise. You're the best."

"I know," she acknowledged, cheerfully.

Sam grinned. Cultural norms might prefer women to be modest, but Elise knew her value, and pretending wasn't her thing.

"Now what do you want me to do about it?" she asked in the next breath.

"Tell Genevieve I need a lift. She can pick me up at the Shaw Recreational Center, corner of 11th Street and Rhode Island Ave, NW." Sam grinned. "Because I'm coming diving with Tom. The *Clarion Call* holds a mystery I intend to personally pry out of her."

CHAPTER FORTY-FOUR

Sam took 11th Street NW out of the terrorist's delineated hot zone section of the capital.

Stopping to search his phone for Alex Goodson's number, he found it and pressed the call button. The phone rang out after several rings. Sam ended the call, then pressed the redial.

Alex picked up on the second ring this time. "Yo! Mr. Reilly. Did you find what you were looking for?"

"You mean, did I find the nuclear bomb hidden in Washington, D.C.?"

"Yeah, that."

"No. But I found something else, which I'm hoping you might clear up for me."

"Shoot."

"There's an old cargo ship which was sunk off the coast of Sandy Point State Park called the *Clarion Call*."

"Yeah?"

"Have you heard of it?"

"No. Should I have?"

"I don't know. It had some significant mechanical issues and was scuttled about five miles off the coast by your father in 1996."

"That would make sense."

"Really? Why?"

"My father was a Major with the 832nd Ordnance Battalion US Marine Corps out of Fort Lee. If the ship was scuttled off the coast of Sandy Point State Park, then it's likely he would've been responsible for sinking it."

"Do you know what year your grandfather and your father stopped speaking to each other?"

"How would I remember that? I was just a kid in 96."

Sam grinned. Alex had answered his questions without actually answering his questions. "I read the FBI's report on you. Apparently, you have an eidetic memory. You were very close to your grandfather, but far from close to your real father. I'm betting a hundred bucks a kid like that would remember when his father and grandfather had a falling out, and prevented you from seeing your grandfather."

"May 22, 1996." Alex sighed heavily. "I never found out what tore them apart. When was the *Clarion Call* scuttled?"

"May 21, 1996."

"Mr. Reilly!"

"Yes?"

"What are you going to do now?"

"I'm going to dive the *Clarion Call* and see if I can find the connection. Then I'm going to pay you another visit."

"Good, you do that." Alex said. "Remember, about a million lives are counting on you."

"Dammit, Alex!" Sam snapped. "I'm the only one here trying to help you. Maybe you should think about that."

CHAPTER FORTY-FIVE

MANHATTAN, NEW YORK

ALEX HUNG UP the phone and walked out onto his balcony. The city spread out in front of him, as busy as an anthill in the early afternoon. He was hungry. Ironically, he'd forgotten to eat. He glanced back at the building. It would be some time before he put the finishing touches on the building of his gamer haven.

Still, everything was coming along nicely.

His father's death had changed his life.

The man who had never understood him and who had always seemed to find ways to tear him down had left this world. His death had taken a weight off his shoulders.

The two of them had never been on the same page.

One of the questions that lingered in Alex's mind was, why? Why had his father always seemed to carry some type of grudge against him? Why had it taken his father's death to unlock his grandfather's bequest?

It felt like his father and grandfather had an inexplicable rivalry between them, as if they'd been arguing over the possession of Alex, the son, and the grandson.

His father had wanted Alex to become one thing, his grandfather another.

Neither of them had waited to discover what Alex wanted for

himself.

When he was still alive, Alex's grandfather openly demonstrated his love for him much more than his father did. Sometimes, his grandfather had sad eyes. He seemed filled with secret regrets, but essentially, he was a man who was satisfied with the way he'd lived his life.

Not so, his father.

He'd seemed consumed with anger from Alex's earliest memories, until his relatively early death. What if he'd lived longer? What would he have done? What if William had left his fortune to Alex before his father's death?

Would Sam Reilly's dive reveal the truth?

He turned away from the balcony, switched his TV back on, and continued to play his game. The troops on both sides of the battle appeared restless.

There would not be a prolonged siege.

The invaders were already setting up their tanks and preparing to storm his fortress. The question of how many lives would be lost in the process remained to be seen.

He selected five of his soldiers. Into his gaming microphone he said, "Prepare the Theodore Roosevelt Bridge for demolition."

"Sir?" the mercenary replied.

"Wire it up. I'm hoping we won't have to use it. But right now, it looks likely."

"Understood."

Everything still depended on Sam Reilly's next move.

Alex grinned.

At least he had chosen the right man to play his game.

CHAPTER FORTY-SIX

ON BOARD THE MARIA HELENA—
TEN MILES EAST OF OCEAN CITY, DELAWARE

THE SEA KING helicopter hovered directly above the *Maria Helena*, as the ship swayed in four feet of gently rolling swell. At the pilot controls next to Sam, Genevieve adeptly maneuvered the large helicopter onto the small helipad to the aft of the vessel.

The familiar sight of his ship brought a smile to Sam's face.

The helicopter's skids touched down on the helipad and Genevieve powered down. Sam unclipped his harness, removed his headphones, and stepped out while the rotors continued to whine overhead.

Matthew, his skipper, greeted him with a firm handshake. "How are you holding up?"

"I'm all right," Sam said, continuing his steady stride across the deck. "Better now that I have something to work on."

Matthew raised a concerned eyebrow. "What are the odds? Do you think the terrorist will go through with the detonation?"

"No."

"But you're worried what you'll find hidden inside the *Clarion Call?*"

Sam nodded. "Worse than that. I'm worried the terrorist

might not be able to stop what he's begun."

"I can imagine that you have every agency in the United States working to assist you." Matthew glanced at Genevieve, who was securing the Sea King to the helipad. "As you know, everyone on board is at your disposal—willing to do anything that you need to get the job done."

"I had no doubts, but thank you anyway." Sam stopped at a portal, ran his eyes across the deck, toward the bridge. "Where are you up to?"

Matthew said, "We've settled directly above the *Clarion Call*. Tom's located her hull on the bathymetric sonar."

Sam exhaled. He didn't expect them to have trouble locating the ship, but it was still a relief. One less thing to go wrong. "Where are Tom and Veyron?"

"They're both down below, preparing the two atmospheric diving suits for the dive."

"All right," Sam said. "I'll join them there and we'll dive as soon as the suits are ready."

"Understood." Matthew paused. "Any idea what you're hoping to find down there?"

Sam grinned. "Answers."

CHAPTER FORTY-SEVEN

SAM QUICKLY STEPPED down the two flights of stairs into the dive room, which was housed between the *Maria Helena's* large twin hulls. Built into the *Maria Helena's* hull the moon pool looked more like something out of an old James Bond movie. Aside from looking cool, it served a much more useful purpose. It allowed for an easy — all weather — dive platform from which to launch a variety of high tech submersibles and SCUBA missions.

To the western edge of the moon pool, stood two large atmospheric diving suits. To Sam's mind, they more closely resembled space suits out of a 1960s science fiction movie, than the highly practical deep-sea diving machines they were.

Veyron removed his diagnostic tools from the internal computer, and looked up to greet him. "Welcome back, Sam."

"Thanks. Where are you at?"

"They're both right to go."

"Great," Sam said. "Where's Tom?"

"He's just having a bite to eat. He'll be down in a minute."

"Ah." Sam grinned. "Everything's normal. Washington D.C. is under threat of a nuclear bomb and Tom's worried about his stomach."

Tom entered the room holding two sandwiches. "It's about keeping my energy up, so we can continue to fight the good fight," he said, walking the steps. He held up two wrapped sandwiches. "I thought you might be hungry, too. You want one?"

"Thanks, Tom. Come to mention it, I haven't eaten in twelve hours."

Ravenous, Sam took the sandwich, devouring it quickly.

His eyes turned to the giant atmospheric diving suits. The new suits were a recent acquisition for the company to replace their previous, older model diving suits. They were custom made by Nuytco Research Ltd in Vancouver, and based on their Exosuit model. The two Exosuits were designed to match Sam and Tom's individual body shapes. Tom's Exosuit was nearly seven-foot-eight inches in height, while Sam's was a little closer to six-foot-four.

Each one provided an articulated submersible of anthropomorphic form which resembled a suit of armor, with elaborate pressure joints to allow freedom of movement while maintaining an internal pressure of one atmosphere. They could be used for very deep dives of up to 1000 feet. Unlike the standard product, these were designed to work autonomously, without an umbilical.

The suits eliminated the majority of physiological dangers associated with deep-sea diving. The occupant need not decompress, there is no need for special gas mixtures, and there is no danger of decompression sickness or nitrogen narcosis.

To be classified as an A1 submersible, the life support systems must last at least 72 hr. Nuytco timed the Exosuit's duration at over 85 hr.

The suit keeps pressure from getting to its occupant with a combination of rigidity and flexibility. The Exosuit is covered in an A356-T6 aluminum alloy skin cast to an average thickness of 0.375 in. Thicker ribs support high-stress areas of the suit. The suit is cast into molds that can also accommodate titanium alloys that withstand greater working depths.

The suit's automatic life support system was fully self-contained. It even provided the occupant with food, water and the ability to excrete bodily waste through a system comparable to that used by astronauts. Additionally, the integrated quad thruster system allowed the pilot to navigate easily underwater, while the hydraulic powered limbs allowed equal maneuverability and strength while out of the water.

In other words, they were cutting edge awesome.

Behind the two behemoth diving suits, lay a small hyperbaric chamber—a solemn and constant reminder of the risks faced with deep sea diving.

Sam finished his sandwich and glanced at Tom, who'd not only consumed his meal, but had also managed to down a large bottle of water in the process.

"All right," Sam said. "Are you good to go?"

"Always," Tom confirmed.

Sam looked at Veyron—who maintained their array of submersible machines. "Are you happy?"

"To let you and Tom out for a play with my two babies?" Veyron asked. "Never. But they're fully prepared to dive. Just don't forget they cost the company a little over half a million dollars apiece."

Sam laughed. "Hey, I signed the check. I doubt I'll forget."

Tom said, "Do you have any idea where we should be looking?"

"Yeah, according to my father, the *Clarion Call's* secret smuggler's compartment would have been located amidships, well below the water-line. The idea was that the secret compartment would be filled with whatever contraband was intended to be shipped while the ship was empty and rode high in the water. Then, after she was loaded with her legal cargo, that compartment would rest beneath the waterline."

Tom smiled. "And the water pressure would in turn, seal this hidden hatch, so that no amount of force could cajole it to open until the main cargo was offloaded. At that point, the ship was high enough that the compartment was above the waterline again."

"Exactly."

It took nearly twenty minutes for each of them to climb inside their respective diving suits, secure their harnesses, lock their watertight seals, and run-through the start-up procedure using a check-list that made piloting a helicopter seem simple.

Then, one by one, Veyron lowered each of the advanced atmospheric diving machines into the water.

Sam watched as the seawater rushed over the dome-shaped viewing port. A moment later, he released the tether, and took control of his submersible.

CHAPTER FORTY-EIGHT

SAM ADJUSTED THE ballast, slowly taking in water until the heavily modified Exosuit became negatively buoyant. At a depth of thirty feet, he brought it back to neutral buoyancy. Beside him, Tom did the same.

He ran his eyes across a series of gauges, confirming that his power and life-support systems were all functioning correctly. Happy with the results, he depressed his radio microphone and said, "How are you looking, Tom?"

The Exosuit used a combination of UQC and 27 KHZ Acoustic which were heterodyned. This was a radio technique used to shift an inputted frequency from one to another through modulation in order to achieve successful transmission—to a high pitch radio frequency for acoustic transmission through water.

"Everything's looking good," came Tom's reply. "You ready to descend?"

"Yeah, I'm good. All right, I'm starting my descent, now."

Sam opened the ballast tanks, and water flooded in while large air bubbles were expelled, until his Exosuit began its continuous descent to the seabed below. The clear surface water rapidly turned into a cloudy darkness.

A small school of large, silvery fish, swam by. At first, Sam instinctively made a sharp turn away from them, as though expecting them to be a large predator. Then, realizing that the

Exosuit offered no harm, turned again to brush by, making a cursory examination. After thirty or so seconds, having discovered nothing to reward their curiosity, the fish disappeared.

Sam glanced at his depth gauge.

They were already at a depth of two hundred and fifty feet.

At four hundred feet, an underwater current carrying debris made their world turn to near complete darkness.

He switched on his overhead LED lights, providing a thick stream of light ahead. Next to him, he spotted Tom's lights pop on. Sam glanced across at his depth gauge. They were coming up on five hundred feet. His eyes turned to the bathymetric sonar array, which gave a colored delineation of the seabed far below.

At six-hundred-feet, the seabed became a series of undulating submerged valleys and hills. The crests were at six-hundred, while the troughs were up to seven hundred and fifty feet.

The *Clarion Call* came into view, positioned with its stern within a deep trough, while its bow rose upward near the six-hundred-feet mark.

Figures. Sam grinned, amused by fate.

The secret smuggling compartment was located near the stern, in the deepest part of the ship. Not that it mattered. The Exosuit had a theoretical crush depth of 2000 and could be safely operated without any concern anywhere below a 1000.

Tom said, "I've picked up the wreck of the scuttled *Clarion Call*."

"I see it. We'll head for the stern, and then work our way up until we reach the smuggling compartment."

Thirty seconds later, Sam reached the *Clarion Call's* stern.

He added some gas to the ballast tanks, slowing his rate of descent until he eased to a standstill approximately thirty feet from the seabed.

Both divers studied the wreckage.

Despite its age and time spent at the bottom of the sea, the *Clarion Call* was in good condition. In the early eighties, she was one of the fastest cargo ships on the oceans. Mike Reilly, his grandfather, had happily paid well to ensure her engineering allowed him to beat all other competitors on speed and reliability.

Sam swept his eyes across the hull. Despite a thin layer of rust, the bulk of the ship was still in perfect condition, listing thirty degrees to her starboard side. Two large openings to the stern showed where the dedicated soldiers from the 832nd Ordnance Battalion US Marine Corps, under the command of Major Roger Goodson, had planted C4 to scuttle the ship.

Tom said, "Tell me the hatch to the secret compartment was on the portside."

"We're good. It's on the portside."

Sam placed slightly greater pressure on the balls of his feet, triggering the Exosuit's quad thrusters to move him toward amidships, while maintaining his upright position. It didn't take long to reach the opening.

The giant hatch — roughly ten feet high by five wide — looked like it had maintained its structural integrity as the *Clarion Call* went to the bottom, until the external pressure became too great, and the door imploded.

Sam glanced inside and hoped to hell whatever secrets once stored inside hadn't been destroyed in the process.

The opening was large enough that they could both comfortably maneuver their large Exosuits inside the remnants of the smuggler's compartment.

Sam adjusted his position and the quad-thrusters whirred into life, sending him inside. He flashed a beam of light around the room. The crumpled remains of the once hidden hatchway were located straight ahead, but the rest of the twenty feet by forty feet vault, appeared empty.

His mouth went dry as his heart sped up. Had he got it all

wrong or had someone retrieved the secrets he needed so desperately?

Over his headset, he heard Tom say, "I think I just found what we were looking for."

CHAPTER FORTY-NINE

Tom stared at the ghastly remains of the man at the corner of the smuggler's vault.

He wore a dark business suit and what appeared to be a red necktie, but after nearly two decades, all that remained of his fleshly body was his skeleton and the scatterings of loose bones. Still attached to what appeared to be an ulna or possibly a radius bone — one of the two lower arm bones — was a locked handcuff and chain, that was attached to a small metallic suitcase.

"What do you want to bet the answers you're looking for are contained within that?" Tom asked, floating toward the metallic suitcase.

"I'll take that bet," Sam replied.

Without further discussion, Sam manipulated his titanium pincers at the end of his right arm and pulled the case free from the bones.

Tom laughed. "All right, you beat me to it."

He adjusted increased opposing power to his twin thrusters, causing him to rotate slowly through three-hundred-and-sixty-degrees. Running his eyes across the room, it appeared almost entirely empty.

When he was finished, he heard Sam say, "Find anything else?"

"No."

"All right, let's head to the surface and find out what was so important inside this case that someone was willing to terrorize Washington, D.C. just to retrieve it."

Tom maneuvered his way through the smuggler's vault and into the open waters outside. Once outside the sunken wreckage, he and Sam added small increments of gas to their ballast tanks.

The two Exosuits began their controlled ascent to the surface.

It was a slow and measured ride. Soon the dark gray of the bottom gave way to the soft light of predawn. Sam kept his eyes fixed on a series of gauges. There were significant external differences between 700 feet and sea level. Even the Exosuit needed to treat that pressure gradient with respect.

Both thinking hard, Sam and Tom rose in silence.

At 500 feet Sam said, "I can't even imagine what that poor man went through. He must've known what happened as soon as he heard the explosions. He knew he was on his way to the bottom, but there wasn't a thing he could do. The external water pressure made it impossible to enter or exit the smuggler's cabin until the cargo was offloaded and the hatch was once more above the waterline."

Tom swallowed. "It would have been a rotten way to go."

"I only hope that whatever secrets are hidden within this suitcase are worth it. Maybe, the stranger's death might not have been in vain."

"Yeah. We'll find out soon."

The gray water turned light, as crepuscular beams shone through the last two hundred or so feet of water.

Tom raised the faceplate of his suit, studying the outline of the *Maria Helena* riding on the surface high above them. His jaw leveled, and his eyes ran across a series of gauges. They had little more than a hundred and fifty feet.

And then his world went dark.

He looked up again and spotted the cause. A large submarine

nearly the length of two football fields and as wide as a three-lane highway had come to a complete stop in the silence directly above them.

Five individual lights suddenly pierced the now pitch-dark canvas.

Sam swore, and said, "It looks like we've got company."

CHAPTER FIFTY

SAM SHOUTED, "LET'S go!"
He pressed all his weight on the balls of his feet, triggering his quad-thrusters into life. He stretched out horizontally, making his bulky Exosuit as streamlined as possible. An instant later, all four propellers whirred, and the suit raced through the water like an uncoordinated torpedo.

They needed to get around the massive submarine to reach the surface.

Above, a set of LED lights raced toward them.

There was no doubt in Sam's mind about their intentions. Their attackers were using weighted sleds to descend at speed.

"We're not going to reach the edge of that sub before they do!" Tom warned.

Sam's head snapped back. The team of elite soldiers were nearly on top of them. "Okay our suits should provide the protection we need, but we can't let them swarm us. Their numbers are overwhelming."

"Agreed. Let's split up. You go left I'll go right."

"Got it!"

Sam put pressure on his left foot and the Exosuit raced diagonally to the left.

The divers didn't stop to rearrange their attack. Instead, they fixed on Sam like a homing missile and kept coming. There was nothing for it. Sam adjusted his position again to a right angle with the sub, in an attempt to shorten the distance.

It didn't matter.

They kept coming.

Sam cleared the imaginary line that formed beneath the edge of the submarine. He dropped his emergency ballast weights. His buoyancy changed in an instant.

The Exosuit shot upward.

It lasted less than a few seconds before he heard the loud clank. One of the divers had landed directly onto the back of his Exosuit. The attacker somehow attached his heavy diving sled to Sam's mechanical leg.

The additional weight had brought Sam to a standstill. He tried to kick it off, but it wouldn't fall free. Sam tried to bend down and reach it. The diver had wrapped a small tether around the base of his left foot. Sam attempted to lift his knee to bring it higher. It felt like he was wearing a cement boot.

Sam said, "Tom, they've got me!"

"I'm coming for you!" came Tom's reply.

"No! Get topside and get help!"

"Not on your life!"

Sam strained the fully articulated joints around his torso and lower abdomen. The suit provided surprising flexibility, but there was limited dexterity, compared to the divers outside who wore nothing but wetsuits and SCUBA. Besides, he only had the use of his left pincer arm — the right was still holding the metallic case.

The metallic case!

The thought snapped him out of his mental cloudiness. He dropped the weighted tether. There was nothing he could do about it right now. Instead, his eyes fixed on the end of his right arm, where the pincer gripped the heavy chain at the end of the metallic case.

Already, one of the divers was trying to pry it free.

Sam rotated his left arm. The fully actuated joints moved quickly, at speeds only just slower than someone outside of the suit. He extended the titanium pincer grip wide and drove his arm toward his attacker.

The pincer collided with the side diver's solar plexus.

Sam squeezed his finger and the pincer closed together. His attacker screamed — or at least he would have, if that had been possible with his dive regulator in his mouth — instead it came out more of a high-pitched gurgle. The diver spun around, recovering faster than Sam had expected. The mechanical force would have crushed any flesh within its way but must have missed any vital organs.

Behind him, his shoulder plate started to move backward.

Someone else had joined their fight, followed by another person at his right. He could hear a slight tapping behind his suit. It was impossible to visualize it, but that didn't matter. He didn't need to. The sound alone was enough to panic him.

Someone was trying to unbolt his helmet!

His pulse racing, Sam jammed the quad-thrusters into full. Their small propellers sped with a whine, but he didn't move far. He was being held by at least four separate divers. Like prehistoric peoples banding together to take down a Woolly Mammoth, his fortified suit would only hold them off so long.

Someone jammed metal into one of his thrusters. It stopped with a loud bang, the noise racing through the water like the sound of his lifeline shattering. The diver immediately worked his way through the rest of the thrusters.

Sam didn't have long to go.

He swung his mechanical arms around like lethal weapons. Every time his arm connected with anything he closed the titanium pincer.

It didn't matter. None of it did. There was no way he could hold off all five of them on his own.

What happened to Tom? Had he changed his mind and continued to the surface for help?

Sam didn't have to wonder very long to find out.

The diver in front of him was suddenly drawn downward. Sam couldn't see what had taken him, but he could guess. Three seconds later, air bubbles raced to the surface, followed by a diver.

Sam cocked his head to the left, and the small crease of a smile curved his lips. It appeared Tom had ripped the diver's regulators straight off the tank. The diver, unable to breathe, had raced toward the surface.

His odds just improved. A lot.

The sight boosted Sam on and he moved his massive, mechanical right leg into a second diver. The knee connected to the man's solar plexus. It should have been enough to knock the man out, or at the very least, take the wind out of his lungs. But instead, the man spun round, and continued to hack at the weaker joints and seals joining Sam's upper torso and his helmet.

A sharp light hiss came from someplace he couldn't see. It was the diver behind him. Whatever the man had been trying to achieve, it looked like he was getting dangerously close.

Sam tugged his legs into his chest and tumbled backward, like a gymnast doing a back summersault.

The diver hung on throughout the maneuver, but when Sam was coming back up, Tom ripped the man's dive-mask clear off — crushing it in one piece, blinding the diver.

"Thanks," Sam said.

Tom replied. "Not a problem. I got bored waiting for you to deal with them and catch up."

They adjusted their positions so that their backs faced each other. The remaining two divers appeared to circle them, never quite coming close enough to confront them, more simply biding their time, waiting for something to happen.

Sam fought with the weight attached to his left boot, but every time he got close to it, one of the divers would make a move, attempting to re-engage.

Stalemate.

In front of them, a second team of divers spewed forth from the submarine. They moved in on them, quickly.

"We gotta go, Sam!" Tom said, "We've got company!"

"I see them!"

Sam tried his weight again, but it didn't budge. Whatever the divers had used to attach it with, was too tough to break, and too flexible to snap. What was worse, with the single pincer it was impossible to untie.

The new group of divers joined what remained of the first and they slowly encroached on Sam and Tom. Again, their opponents appeared to work with the smooth and lethal efficiency of elite forces.

Every time one of them got within arm's reach, Sam or Tom would try to punch or kick them. They were able to move surprisingly fast for two guys in giant atmospheric suits. More importantly, weighing nearly 500 pounds meant that if they connected with their target, it would serve its purpose well.

None of the divers had a weapon, or if they did, none of them wanted to use it. That was interesting. It meant they weren't interested in killing him — yet.

So what did they want to do, abduct him?

The Mexican standoff continued for at least fifteen minutes, with neither side gaining any real advantage. Their attackers had more men, but Sam and Tom had a much larger air supply. If they could hold off for another thirty minutes, the divers would almost certainly run out of air.

Everything was going to be all right.

That was until someone managed to cut Tom's emergency ballast weights.

CHAPTER FIFTY-ONE

FREE FROM ITS iron emergency ballast, Tom's Exosuit raced toward the surface. He tried to fight his extreme buoyancy by swimming downward, but it was impossible. He was simply too positively buoyant.

His Exosuit broached the surface and warm sun hit his face full on.

He was on the VHF radio to the *Maria Helena* in an instant. "Pull me up, Sam's being kidnapped!"

"Kidnapped?" came Matthew's calm reply. "We've taken two diver's hostage ourselves. They're on deck now, but don't seem interested in talking."

Genevieve was in the water a moment later, hooking up the tether for the crane. Veyron started to bring Tom in.

Tom said, "Tell Elise to get the Secretary of Defense on the line and keep her there. I want to speak to her the second I'm on board."

"Understood," Matthew replied.

The crane extended several feet off the starboard side of the *Maria Helena's* deck. Tom heard the machine's diesel engine kick into action. The engine whined as Veyron knocked it into gear, and the cable started to shift.

A moment later, Tom was being lifted into the air by a steel tether attached to the top of the atmospheric diving suit. At a height of roughly ten feet above the sea, the crane rotated until the Exosuit was directly above the deck. Then Veyron kicked the winch into the opposite direction.

Tom's feet reached the deck of the *Maria Helena*. He felt unsteady. The suit wasn't designed for movement on land — it was only stable in the water. Genevieve secured the back of the atmospheric diving suit to a holding cradle, and Veyron quickly went to work removing Tom's helmet.

As soon as it was off, Elise handed him the satellite phone.

Tom said, "Madam Secretary?"

"What happened Tom?"

"One of your subs just kidnapped Sam!"

"You sure it was one of our submarines?" she asked, her voice terse.

"Certain. It was the heavily modified Seawolf Class Nuclear attack submarine, the *USS Jimmy Carter*."

"The Jimmy Carter..." she let the words slowly roll off her tongue. "Are you sure? How the hell could you possibly recognize her?"

"For starters, it was the last of the Seawolf Class nuclear attack submarines. It had nearly a hundred feet in greater length that allowed for the insertion of an additional section known as the Multi-Mission Platform, which allowed launch and recovery of ROVs and Navy SEAL forces. In this case, that was how they kidnapped Sam." Tom sighed. "And besides, I read the number on the conning tower — 23 — AKA *USS Jimmy Carter* SSN-23."

"You've memorized every submarine by number?" she asked, without shielding her scepticism.

"No. My dad commanded her two years during her original sea trials."

"Okay," she accepted the fact. "Assuming you're right and its one of our subs that have kidnapped Sam, why would they do so? He's on our side."

Tom said, "Sure, but are they?"

"Are you questioning the loyalty of the men and women on board one of our nuclear attack subs?"

"Not at all, ma'am. Having served myself, I wouldn't dream of it. My concern is with senior brass and politicians who might be willing to kill to protect whatever secrets were buried inside the *Clarion Call*."

The Secretary of Defense paused, as though considering the possibility. "But who would even know that Sam was planning on diving the *Clarion Call* today?"

"Exactly. Sam Reilly informed you that we planned to dive her and retrieve whatever was buried inside old man Mike Reilly's secret smuggling compartment. Who did you tell?"

The phone went quiet. Suddenly, she swore. "I informed the Chairman of the Joint Chiefs of Staff, who is currently with the President inside the Presidential Emergency Operations Center."

"Who would he have informed?" Tom persisted.

"Good God!"

"What?"

"The President, naturally, but also each of the Military Service Chiefs from the Army, Marine Corps, Navy, and Air Force, and the Chief of the National Guard Bureau."

"And now we have an abduction by a nuclear attack submarine, while Sam tried to retrieve secrets from the scuttled *Clarion Call*."

"Did he find what he was looking for?" she asked.

"Yes, and now they have it."

"Then there's nothing we can do. It's unlikely they will kill him. The submariners probably have orders to retrieve the evidence, and then they will return him to the nearest dock."

"Or they will kill him to stop him from talking."

"Either way there's nothing I can do for you from here. If I challenge the Chief of the Navy, and he's culpable, he will refute it. And if he's not involved, but someone down his chain of command is responsible, then it will only increase their need to eliminate the evidence by killing Sam."

"So that's it then?" Tom asked.

"I'm sorry, Tom. My hands are tied."

"Okay, but mine aren't."

Tom ended the call. His eyes fixed on Genevieve and Veyron who'd been listening to the hurried conversation. Their hardened resolve, expressed exactly what he was thinking — *the crew of the Maria Helena never left anyone behind.*

Genevieve said, "All right. How do you want to play this thing?"

"We're going to have to retrieve Sam ourselves."

Matthew stared at him, a mixture of disbelief and astonishment in his sky-blue eyes. "You've got to be kidding. How?"

Tom grinned sardonically. "By boarding their submarine."

CHAPTER FIFTY-TWO

After one of the divers severed Tom's emergency ballast weights and sent him skyrocketing to the surface, there was nothing Sam could do to overcome the remaining seven attackers. Within minutes, they had disabled him, binding his pincers together so that they could no longer open them and wreak havoc on their soft flesh.

Unable to do anything to prevent it, he was dragged in through the submarine's Multi-Mission Platform, which allowed launch and recovery of ROVs and Navy SEAL forces. He'd seen them on other submarines but was surprised to learn that his attackers had been Navy SEALs.

Once inside the lockout chamber, the outer hatch was sealed and the water vented, leaving them inside a dry chamber. The elite soldiers worked quickly with a set of spanners to remove his atmospheric diving suit.

As soon as they pulled off his large helmet, they dragged Sam through the opening. He provided little resistance. He was trapped in a confined space with four U.S. Navy SEALs, there wasn't just little chance that he could escape—there was no chance he could escape. Besides, it was unlikely they wanted him dead. If they had, he'd little doubt he would be dead already.

Sam shot one of the men a faint grin. "No, no, gentlemen. I'm sure I said pick me up at eight for prom night."

One of the shorter SEALs made a thin-lipped smile, clearly unimpressed by Sam's bravado. "Cute."

Sam met his steely gaze. "All right, let's cut to the chase. Which one of you want to tell me why I'm here?"

"Mr. Sam Reilly, my name is A.J." the shorter SEAL replied. "And you're here, because you couldn't help sticking your nose where it didn't belong. Some secrets were meant to stay buried, for the good of this country. You of all people should know that."

Sam shook his head. "There are systems in place for matters of national security. If that was the case, this situation would never have gotten to where it is now."

"Those systems were in place. And those secrets weren't supposed to ever reach the light of day. You've no idea how many lives you put at risk."

"I don't know if you know this, A.J." Sam's lips tried to form a reassuring smile, but they were struggling to find anchorage. "I'm acting under orders from the Secretary of Defense, so whoever it is you're upset about, it's not me."

A.J. remained silent. Sam couldn't tell whether the man hadn't heard him correctly or was choosing to ignore him.

The second hatch opened.

A.J. smiled. "Welcome aboard the *USS Jimmy Carter*. This is commander Dylan Brooks."

Sam's eyes drifted down the ladder, landing on a surly man of approximately forty-five years old. He stood with the solid confident authority of one who'd spent plenty of time in command.

"Sam Reilly?"

"Yes, sir."

"I'm commander Brooks." Brooks ran his eyes across his prisoner. "You've no idea how much damage you've caused today, have you, son?"

"No, sir," Sam replied. He'd been in the marines a long time ago, and met the commander's type before. There was no logical reason to get into an argument with him.

"Well. What do you have to say for yourself?"

Sam exhaled a deep breath. "You know there's a terrorist holding Washington, D.C. to ransom with a World War II German nuclear bomb, don't you? He's targeted me, for reasons that I don't understand, to play a game with him. Diving the *Clarion Call* was part of that game."

The commander shook his head in disgust. "Son, you have no idea what game's being played here."

"So what is being played here?"

The commander's eyes narrowed. "Someone has you digging into secrets — dangerous secrets — that were never meant to be revealed."

Sam said, "Sometimes the truth is important."

"And sometimes it's dangerous as hell. When it comes to national security, the human race is too important to be trifled with over honesty," the commander countered.

Sam kept his mouth shut. He could see this conversation had no chance of going anywhere he hoped it might go.

The commander turned to A.J. "We need to get underway. What's taking so long?"

One of the SEALs apologized. "Sorry, sir. I lost three men back there after their air supplies were destroyed. They swam to the surface. I've sent the rescue unit out to retrieve them. They won't be long."

"Understood. Let me know as soon as they're inside. I've orders to take Sam Reilly to the Joint Base Anacostia-Bolling. There is someone who needs to speak to him in private, right away."

Sam was handcuffed, his wrists in front of him.

A.J. said, "Sorry, but a nuclear submarine can be a dangerous place to let a man loose."

Sam nodded. "I understand. Some might have thought it would have been easier to not bring me in at all?"

"Nothing personal," A.J. replied. "We've got our orders."

Sam said, "Sure. And I have mine."

A.J. ignored him, disappearing down a separate gangway, while a SEAL lead Sam down the gangway and into the junior officer's quarters. Two guards stood at the doorway. Sam stretched out on one of the small beds. It might be a long wait, may as well get some rest.

He closed his eyes. It had been nearly twenty-four hours since this thing had begun, and he hadn't stopped. He was so dead tired, nothing could keep him awake much longer.

Outside his makeshift prison, someone made the comment, "They're inside the flooded lockout chamber now."

"Good," came the curt reply. "I'll order us underway, while they blow the water. No reason to delay our meeting at Joint Base Anacostia–Bolling."

Sam was nearly asleep—his heavily burdened mind, giving way to fatigue. In the back of his mind, he heard footsteps move quickly down the lockout chamber's ladder. Those same footsteps moved quickly toward his make-shift prison.

A commanding voice that sounded vaguely familiar, asked, "Where are you holding Sam Reilly?"

"Who are you?" came the startled reply.

"No one you wanna mess with," Tom answered. "Now where are you keeping Sam Reilly?"

"I don't know what you're talking about."

Gunshots followed.

Several shots in rapid succession. Most likely fired by an MP5 submachinegun. Followed by the sound of boots on the metal grate that formed the platform, echoed down the narrow confines of the gangway.

That was enough to make Sam sit up. "I'm here!"

Tom hunched his large frame under a solid bulkhead. "Ah, there you are. We've been waiting for ages for you to finish up down here and make your way to the surface."

Sam shot out of his borrowed bed. "Sorry to keep you waiting."

"No problem. Normally you're pretty reliable," Tom observed.

"Thanks, Tom."

Reaching the door, his eyes swept the gangway, where Veyron and Genevieve were guarding both directions with MP5 submachineguns. The three of them wore the wetsuits used by the Navy SEALs who'd been forced to surface earlier. Each one had the name of the SEAL written into the wetsuit. His eyes set toward amidships, where a large bulkhead door was slammed shut — blocking their passage to the lockout chamber.

CHAPTER FIFTY-THREE

SAM RACED TO the wheel-lock, with Tom.

The two of them tried in a vain attempt to open the bulkhead door. It had been secured somehow from the opposing side. There was nothing they could do about it. The door was several inches thick and designed to withstand the enormous pressures of external seawater in the event of a hull breach.

Genevieve sent a couple rounds down the gangway heading toward the stern, preventing anyone from attempt to close the next bulkhead door.

Veyron politely said, "Genevieve. You know we all love you, but you are on board a nuclear submarine, and I would be most obliged if you at least attempted to refrain from firing bullets!"

Genevieve gave him a coy smile. "I'll try my best."

Tom said, "That's all you can do, dear."

Someone's hand reached for the bulkhead door. A single shot fired, putting a hole in the middle of the hand. The person behind the door cursed, his footsteps running further aft.

Sam looked at Genevieve like a disappointed parent. "What did we just talk about?"

She shrugged with indifference. "What?"

Stepping back from the bulkhead door, Sam asked Tom, "What's your plan B?"

"We've got to get to the stern," Tom said, gripping his MP5. "There's an emergency lock-out trunk we can take to the surface. If we can get there."

Genevieve grinned. "We'll get there."

Tom said, "The crew of the USS *Jimmy Carter* won't have weapons yet. There's a small arms locker near the command center. They will be quickly arming themselves, but we shouldn't have too much resistance on our way to the stern."

They moved quickly, racing down the narrow passageways.

Sam cleared the second bulkhead door and closed it behind him. Up ahead, Tom was securing the ante chamber to the lock-out escape trunk.

He took a step forward and stopped.

A shotgun blast pelted the submarine's hull right in front of him. It most likely came from one of the Navy's Remington 12 pump action, designed to achieve maximum damage within the confined fighting quarters of a submarine. It was a last line of defense, used to repel boarders.

Sam dropped to the ground. His head snapping round to the right, where the shot was fired. It was coming from the sub's cook compartment.

What is it with Navy cooks and die-hard heroes?

Sam shouted, "We don't want any trouble."

Silence.

"We just want to get off the sub."

More silence.

He needed to get past the small opening, and keep moving aft, if they were going to escape. Problem was, to do so, would involve passing directly in front of a submariner with a shotgun. His likelihood of surviving was insurmountable.

Next to him, a large spanner was attached to the wall — an emergency tool to shut off any water or gas pipes in the event of a hull breach.

He picked up the heavy tool and threw it in front of the opening.

Another shotgun blast.

Followed by the sound of the spanner hitting the metal flooring of the gangway.

Sam felt his heart race. His breathing quick and ragged.

"Genevieve!" he shouted. "I might need some help here."

Her eyes were flat. "We're working on it, Sam."

Genevieve and Tom took cover on the opposite end, securing the aft section of the submarine, while Veyron prepared the lockout-trunk for an emergency escape. Genevieve closed the next bulkhead door, freeing herself up to return to help Sam.

She leaned in close to the entrance of the kitchen. It was a narrow slit, barely large enough for a big person to get into. The cook — if it even was a cook — had positioned himself all the way at the back, at least ten feet. That meant Genevieve would need to reveal her own position, making herself vulnerable if she hoped to place a shot downrange.

What made matters worse, no one had any intention of killing the submariner. Like Sam said, they just needed to get by and escape.

Sam said, "We need a diversion."

"We're working on it," Tom said.

Veyron climbed back down from the lockout trunk. His eyes darted around the room with curiosity. A wry smile formed on his lips and his normally impassive face, livened with fascinated interest as though he were trying to resolve a complex engineering puzzle. His eyes darted around the room until he spotted the spanner. He stepped over and picked it up. "Someone say a diversion?"

Sam grinned. "Yeah, what are you thinking?"

Veyron stared at a series of pipes that ran along the metal wall of the interior hull. He tapped one of the pipes. It made a dull, hollow sound. He tapped a second one. This one made more of a sharp, higher pitched sound. He glanced at the names of each valve.

They were clearly labeled so that, in the event of a hull breach, any submariner could identify them easily so that they could be operated.

Veyron shined his flashlight on one labeled: Kingston Valves — Bow.

Next to that was another one labeled: Ballast Air Vents — Bow

He shined his flashlight down farther, until he spotted the same two corresponding valves for the aft tank.

Sam watched as Veyron used the spanner to set the aft vents into the closed position, while opening the air vent in the bow. During normal operation, the Kingston valve was used to admit seawater into the ballast tank. Once the submarine had dived, the Kingston valve could remain open, while the closed air vent kept any further influx of seawater to the ballast tanks by the pressure of trapped air.

When Veyron opened the bow air vent, the forward ballast became quickly flooded with water.

A moment later, he vented gas into the aft ballast.

The effect on the submarine's trim was immediate. The bow began to sink, while the stern rose sharply. The bow dipped forward at a twenty-eight-degree dive. The submarine instantly started to creak, as the reinforced steel accommodated the change in hull-pressure.

Sam gripped the side of the gangway to prevent himself from falling. Inside the kitchen, he heard the resounding crunch of the cook's body — surrounded by smooth hygienic metal — slip and fall.

He didn't wait for another chance. Sam quickly climbed across the opening, catching up with Veyron, Tom, and Genevieve.

Tom took a deep breath. "Told you we'd sort it out. Try not to lag behind next time, okay?'

"I'll do my best." Sam turned to Veyron. "What the hell are you doing?"

Veyron smiled. "Distracting them!"

"By sinking the ship?" Sam asked, a hint of desperation in his tone. "There are nearly three hundred American lives on board!"

"It's all right. They have another five hundred feet below their keel. It's plenty of space for our finest to correct the problem with the trim — but it might just buy us enough time to reach the surface."

Tom said, "You're certain your diversion isn't going to sink my dad's first command?"

Veyron nodded, confidently. "Every submariner on board this submarine can read these gauges and will know how to correct it. Nothing's locked out. The venting valves run throughout the entire hull, so that any one of them can be used to correct the problem.

"All right," Sam agreed. "Let's go then before they work it out."

Sam, Tom, Veyron, and finally Genevieve donned the red RFD Beaufort SEIE Mark 11 — AKA submarine escape immersion equipment — and climbed up the ladder into the aft emergency escape lock-out trunk.

Already the submarine had started to level out. Genevieve was the last one up the ladder. Near the kitchen, the bulkhead door opened and one of the submariner's raced through. Tom gripped Genevieve's hand, quickly jerking her into the lock-out trunk.

Veyron closed the water-tight door.

Beneath them, someone tried to open it again, but Tom had already pulled the latch, flooding the small compartment. It filled quickly. When the internal pressure equalized with the outer seawater, the lock-out trunk hatch opened.

All four of them raced to the surface at a rate of roughly ten feet per second. Sam exhaled the entire time.

One by one, all four of them broached the surface of the water, their red SEIE suits ballooning on top of the ocean waves.

Matthew and Elise had plucked all four of them out of the water within minutes, and the *Maria Helena* was soon motoring at full speed to the closest harbor.

Sam grinned. "Thanks for pulling off the impossible. Now let's go find out what in the world this was all about."

Tom sighed heavily. "Sorry we might never know. We couldn't find the metallic case on the *USS Jimmy Carter*. It must be lost for good by now."

Sam laughed long and hard, far too amused for the situation they were in. He asked, "Tom, didn't you notice it before…"

"Notice what?"

"Remember when the SEALs blew your emergency ballast sending you racing to the surface?"

"Of course."

"Before they did, I dropped the case into your carry pouch on the back of your Exosuit. I thought you knew?"

"Nope." It was Tom's turn to smile. "Well, that's good, then. That means it's now time to find the truth."

CHAPTER FIFTY-FOUR

ON BOARD THE MARIA HELENA

SAM EXAMINED THE metallic case. It had been state of the art at the time of the *Clarion Call*'s scuttling. It's titanium alloy was strong and light, keeping the contents well protected from the elements — even at a depth of 700 feet.

He took it to the engineering bay on the second level below deck, his friends following behind him like a row of ducklings. Fixing the case to a workbench using a large vice, Veyron used one of his drilling tools to achieve what two decades on the seabed could not — and opened the case.

There was a single folder, labelled: *Clarion Call. Ship's manifest.*

Sam opened it.

On the first page, was a handwritten note, addressed to a senator named Peter Grzonkowski.

The name sounded familiar to Sam, but he couldn't quite place it.

He read the first line.

> *Dear Senator, Peter Grzonkowski,*
> *As requested, here is the proof you needed.*
> *After you have taken possession of the shipping manifest, I'm going to go to ground and disappear until this thing*

blows over. As you can appreciate, this information is going to upset many powerful people. A lot of people from around the world – including my own brother and our government – are going to want to see blood.

So be careful.

Good luck.

Joseph Finney

Sam opened the binder and quickly ran his eyes across the first few pages. He didn't go far. Instead, he stopped. His heart pounded in his ears, his throat constricted.

The truth was so startling simple, yet shatteringly clear in its validity. The world would never be the same once it was out.

How did the U.S. government think they had a right to withhold this information?

Sam swallowed hard.

More importantly, did he have the right to tell it?

He closed the manifest with a defiant snap, securing the metallic case.

Tom met his eye, and asked, "What is it?"

Sam shook his head. "How did they possibly get away with it so long?"

"What?"

"No wonder the Navy didn't want us to reveal the truth!" Sam said, in awe. Instead of answering Tom, he turned to Elise. "Does the name, Senator Peter Grzonkowski mean anything to you?"

"Do you mean, Congressman Peter Grzonkowski from Illinois?"

"Yeah that might be him." Sam pursed his lips, squeezing his eyes shut. "Where have I heard that name recently?"

Without hesitation, Elise said, "He was with Congresswoman Bledes when she was shot dead, while trying to escape the capital. I believe she was with Congressmen Grzonkowski and

Carmichael at the time, along with three Federal agents."

Sam stood up. "We have to go—now."

"Why?" Elise asked.

Sam's eyes focused on Genevieve. "Genevieve, get the rotor turning on the Sea King."

Genevieve nodded and immediately left, without asking for a reason.

Sam turned to Tom. "Go grab another MP5 for each of us and meet me on the helipad."

Tom said, "I'm on it!"

Elise repeated the question. "Why?"

Sam looked at her determined and fixed violet eyes. "Sorry, Elise. What was the question?"

She smiled. "What does this have to do with Congresswoman Bledes?"

"Absolutely nothing. Congresswoman Bledes was never the target."

"Who was?"

Sam ground his teeth. With a cold, steely voice, he said, "Congressman Peter Grzonkowski."

Elise asked, "Where are you going?"

"To protect the truth!"

"How?"

Sam took a deep breath. "By retrieving the Congressman before someone kills him."

CHAPTER FIFTY-FIVE

THE SEA KING helicopter took off, heading due west, toward Washington, D.C. The sea below appeared calm ultramarine blue with small white ripples, where the *Maria Helena* motored toward Chesapeake Bay. Inside, Sam picked up his cell phone and dialed Alex Goodson's number.

Alex picked up on the first ring. "Hi, Mr. Reilly. How was your dive?"

"Very informative," Sam replied. "Alex, I know the truth. I know what Werner Heisenberg did."

Alex didn't reply, instead there was only the garbled static of his cell phone.

Sam said, "Did you hear me, Alex? I said, I know what Werner Heisenberg did."

"I'm sorry, Sam," Alex said, his voice calm, yet also a bit sad. Almost like a kid being told it was too late to get an ice-cream cone, because the truck had just driven off. "I can't quite hear you. I'm afraid it's probably a bit too late for you to come over and play, anyway. I'm about to finish the game. Thanks for the offer, though."

Sam tasted bile in his throat. His breathing became uneven, his nostrils flared. "It was never about Congresswoman Bledes. They were trying to kill Congressman Peter Grzonkowski! He's the only one who knows the whole truth. They're going to kill him!"

"Who?"

"Peter Grzonkowski!"

"Never heard of him, Sam," Alex said, but there was no conviction in his voice. "I'm sorry, can I call you back? I'm at a really interesting part of my game. I'm afraid those names don't help anymore."

"No. Peter Grzonkowski can make this right!"

"No, he can't. It's too late now. The game's nearly over!"

"Wait!" Sam yelled. "I can fix this."

But it didn't matter. The connection had ended.

Tom worked his way through checking the two MP5 submachineguns they brought with them. He cocked his head to the left and made a wry smile. "That didn't sound like it went too well."

"It didn't."

"What do you want to do about it?"

Sam set his jaw and gripped his MP5. "We're just going to have to save Congressman Grzonkowski ourselves."

CHAPTER FIFTY-SIX

PENTAGON COMMAND CENTER

THE SECRETARY OF Defense stared at the image of Washington, D.C. taken via their high-altitude surveillance drone.

A large contingent of tanks and armored personnel carriers were heading east along the Curtis Memorial Parkway toward the Theodore Roosevelt Bridge. She increased the magnification and noticed that they were accompanied by two teams of special forces.

They are going to attempt to breach the capital!

She picked up the phone—a direct line to the Joint Chiefs of Staff in the Presidential Operational Command Center beneath the White House.

Her eyes fixed on the fast-moving war machines heading toward her capital. A man answered on the first ring. "Yes?"

Normally calm and unruffled, the Secretary was seriously pissed off. Her no-nonsense voice barked, "Who the hell gave the damned order to breach?"

CHAPTER FIFTY-SEVEN

CONGRESSMAN PETER GRZONKOWSKI stared out the giant glass windows.

He was standing on the fourth floor of the United States Peace Institute, where he and his colleagues had taken refuge. He had to laugh at the irony of being bunkered down in such a place during what was shaping up to be potentially the worst attack on U.S. soil since winning Independence from the British Empire on July 4, 1776.

He wasn't afraid to die. His father, a World War II Veteran, had instilled in him the devout and sacred belief, in the doctrine of self-sacrifice and service to his country. With a loving wife, and three children, he certainly didn't seek his demise, but nor was he going to dwell on that which he couldn't control.

Instead, he feared the past—and more importantly, how it would affect the future.

Did someone know that he'd met with Joseph Finney all those years ago?

He closed his eyes, tasting bile in his mouth. He searched his own conscience, and his throat constricted by what he saw. It wasn't fear. It was remorse, for not being true to a friend.

Once Joseph Finney disappeared, all he could do was assume the worst—that someone had killed him to prevent the truth from becoming known. He should have gone on to reveal what he knew. To open up a Congressional Hearing.

But without evidence, what choice did I ever really have?

He opened his eyes and promised himself that if he survived the attack on his nation's capital, he would arrange a full Congressional Inquest into what happened during those dark days at the end of World War II. That was when a new — albeit much more clandestine — war was only just beginning.

His eyes swept the landscape ahead from left to right. The Potomac River glistened in the warm summer's day. Birdlife, blissfully unaware of the troubled world around them, played in the water between the Arlington Memorial Bridge and the Theodore Roosevelt Bridge.

The bridge — normally full of joggers, walkers, and tourists, was now deathly empty.

His view settled on the Curtis Memorial Parkway in the distance and his lips curled into an upward smile. He felt his heart race and exhaled a deep breath, because a large convoy of military vehicles were approaching.

And that meant, the good guys were finally coming.

CHAPTER FIFTY-EIGHT

ALEX GOODSON SAT down at his gaming station.
Was it all, really too late?

He un-paused his game and thought about what Sam Reilly had told him. His breathing was even. His pulse, steady. His eyebrows narrowed as he studied the gaming map toward the top-left hand corner. It provided an almost cartoonish image of a small urban city. The one he focused on was named, Washington, D.C.

His eyes swept the entire map, from Capitol Hill through to the Potomac River, landing on a large convoy of military tanks and armored personnel carriers.

Had it gone too far to quit?

If he'd been normal, his adrenal system would have gone into overdrive at this point. His natural fight or flight response would be taking over, clouding his judgement, and helping him act with sharp and immediate instincts.

But Alex wasn't normal. Never had been. Instead, he felt calm. His piercing blue eyes fixed on the Theodore Roosevelt Bridge with an icy conviction. He adeptly moved his players into place, quickly, setting everything up for whatever may be.

The tanks were getting closer.
There was still time to stop.
From the east, a civilian Sea King helicopter was flying over

Capitol Hill.

Alex sighed.

He was never going to quit. It just wasn't the way he played the game. Never was. He scrolled down on his computer gaming console until he reached what he wanted. It showed a cartoonish image of a coyote depressing a T-shaped dynamite detonator from Wile E. Coyote and the Road Runner.

Alex clicked on the image.

A warning message came up on the screen — ARE YOU SURE YOU WANT TO DETONATE?

Alex grinned and pressed enter.

CHAPTER FIFTY-NINE

The Sea King had her nose angled downward taking off some altitude in preparation for landing. Sam studied the military convoy approaching the Theodore Roosevelt Bridge. *What the hell are they thinking?* He picked up his cell phone and frantically tried to call the Secretary of Defense.

She answered the call, and he didn't wait to speak. "You have to stop the convoy from breaching the city! I need more time!"

"I'm sorry, Sam. There is no more time. I can't stop them. Someone from the Joint Chiefs of Staff has given the order and the President has approved it."

"Alex isn't going to respond well to breaking the rules."

"You still think it's him, don't you?"

"Yes."

"Let's hope you're right," she said. "We have a team of FBI agents working surveillance at his house right now. The kids just playing some stupid computer game."

"Oh yeah, what's the name of the game?"

"How the hell would I know, Sam? Last report, he was playing some sort of nerdy urban warfare game. There was a river and a bridge and tanks…" she broke off mid-sentence and swore. "I've got to get someone to stop him!"

Sam didn't know if the Secretary of Defense was able to get through to the commander of the armored convoy or not, but it no longer mattered. Genevieve spotted the curved sail-shaped roof of the United States Institute of Peace. On the east rooftop, were the speckled shapes of five men. The Secretary of Defense had already told them to expect a ride from the roof.

Genevieve dipped the Sea King's nose, and then brought it to a hover just over the western edge of the roof top. In the back, Tom swung the sliding doors open and one by one each of the four men climbed on board.

"Everyone's in!" Tom shouted.

Genevieve didn't have to be told twice. She pushed her right foot on the anti-torque pedal. The helicopter rotated sharply on its axis, so that her windshield now faced the Potomac.

Sam exhaled a sigh of relief. They had retrieved Congressman Peter Grzonkowski. With him safe, and the secrets he knew capable of exposure, he was confident Alex would withdraw the threat to end the game.

An instant later, there was a loud explosion, followed by many more.

Every bridge along the Potomac through to the Anacostia, from the Francis Scott Key Bridge to the John Phillip Sousa exploded in a mass of fire and debris. The structural roads collapsed.

Next to him, Genevieve opened the Sea King's throttle to full, and yanked the collective up. The helicopter climbed rapidly. Heat from the multiple explosions could be felt through the windshield. Sam ran his eyes across the burning remains of the capital. More than a hundred smaller explosions were taking place.

As the helicopter climbed, he noticed that for the most part, the ordnance set were more for show than actual damage. Throughout the capital buildings, thick purple smoke rose, shrouding the entire area in darkness.

Genevieve set a course for the Pentagon.

Sam looked back over his shoulder. "Congressman Peter

Grzonkowski?"

"Yes, sir," came a congenial reply. "You must be Sam Reilly."

"That's me." Sam beamed with pleasure. "Next to you is Tom, and your pilot today is Genevieve."

The Congressman smiled. "Not that I'm complaining, but I have to ask, why me? Why did you come get me?"

Sam grinned. "I have a letter and a ship's manifest from the *Clarion Call* that's been waiting a long time to reach you."

CHAPTER SIXTY

ALEX GOODSON'S APARTMENT, MANHATTAN

Sam Reilly followed the FBI Special Weapons and Tactics team into the building.

They moved quickly, running up the main stairs at the front and securing the entire building within minutes. Alex Goodson was home by himself. He didn't put up any resistance. In fact, because he was wearing gaming headphones and was absorbed in his video game, he didn't realize that a SWAT team had invaded the privacy of his house until he was in handcuffs.

Alex was already in his pajamas but didn't appear disturbed or surprised by the intrusion of some thirty or more FBI agents. He caught Sam's eye. "Hey, Mr. Reilly, didn't I tell you it was probably too late to play another game?"

"Afraid this isn't about games," Sam replied.

Alex smiled, but wore a vacant expression of insouciance. "Oh yeah. What's this about?"

A federal agent tightened the handcuffs until they dug into Alex's wrist. The young man didn't react. "The terrorist attack on Washington, D.C."

"Hey, you caught someone did you?" Alex looked at Sam. "I always knew you had it in you. You're a smart guy, Mr. Reilly. So, who was the terrorist? I mean, who would do such a terrible thing, like threaten our nation's capital?"

Sam said, "It's not a joke. Lives were lost. Infrastructure was significantly damaged."

Alex shrugged. "I heard that only one life was lost, and that the terrorist wasn't even involved in that one."

"Game's over, Alex. You can cut the crap."

Alex cocked his head to the side. "What crap?"

"The video game you were playing. It wasn't a game was it? It was a real-time projection of your battlefield in Washington, D.C. and those soldiers in your game, weren't just characters, those were the men on the ground who you were giving orders to."

Alex's eyes narrowed, his lips formed into a practiced smile. "You think I was behind the terrorist attack on our capital? You've got to be crazy. I've been here the whole time. You should know, someone had four agents running surveillance on me since this started. One in the van out the front, one on my neighbor's roof, one working on the powerlines, and one in the shop beneath my apartment. So, you see, there was no chance that I could've been involved in anything as far away as Washington, D.C."

Sam moved to the video game controller and switched the TV back on. An urban warfare game was paused. He clicked the unpause button and the came continued to play in real-time. The FBI agents watched for a minute, while Sam maneuvered the gaming console so he could visualize the location.

It was a city with two large rivers, branching off to form a large Y-shape, in the middle of which, a large dome-shaped building rose from a city shrouded in purple smoke. Bridges along both lengths of the two rivers had been razed. Their foundations still smoldered.

All eyes in the room remained on the city.

But it wasn't Washington, D.C. — it was Budapest. As the purple smoke dissipated, it revealed that the domed-building wasn't the Capitol, but the Central Dome of the Hungarian Parliament, and instead of the Potomac, it was the Danube River.

Sam's lips curled into a wry smile. "This doesn't prove anything. You've been playing me all along. You must've changed games. You knew I was coming for you."

Alex shrugged. "If that's what you think. We all make up things from time to time. I particularly have that trouble. The trick is to remember what's real and try and differentiate it from one's imagination."

The FBI agents searched his house from top to bottom. A team of computer hackers from the cyberwarfare division analyzed his gaming set up.

All told, it was nearly midnight before they were complete.

The FBI agent in charge unhandcuffed Alex. "Sir, I'm sorry for the intrusion. All I can say was that we were fed poor intel. Good night."

Sam met the agent's eye. With his arms spread, his palms facing upward, he said, "You've got to be kidding me! I was here! I watched him move his men around, setting up the dynamite that would level the Theodore Roosevelt Bridge."

"No, you didn't," the agent replied. "You saw him setting up an urban battlefield in a game, set in Budapest."

Sam shook his head. "I know what I saw. Besides, I know how Alex thinks. He's been leading me around the city for the past twenty-four hours!"

The agent shrugged. "What can I say? He's clean. His gaming TV isn't even connected to the internet. In fact, his server down below hasn't even been connected to the fiber-optics node yet."

"All right," Sam said. "I could've sworn that it was Washington, D.C."

One by one, each of the Federal Agents left the building.

Sam was the last to leave.

At the door, Alex shook his hand and patted him on the

shoulder paternalistically. "You know what, Mr. Reilly?"

Sam met his gaze with a dimpled smile. "What?"

"Your grandfather was a crook, and your father's not much better, but you're okay. You're okay."

Bemused, Sam shook his head and smiled. "Thanks. Hey Alex…"

"Yeah?"

"What was this all really about?"

"You tell me?" Alex replied. "You were the one trying to investigate a terrorist. I was just playing a game. You're the professional. You take care of yourself, Sam. Don't let Washington and all your other powerful connections corrupt you."

Sam stepped out of the kid's apartment and started walking down the street. He hadn't made it more than a block when his cell phone received a text message. Not his cell phone, but the one the terrorist had given him. He opened the message.

Written on it was a single set of GPS coordinates.

Underneath it, it read:

Thanks for playing the game. A.G.

CHAPTER SIXTY-ONE

THE SECRETARY OF Defense leaned back into her chair inside the Command Center. Her eyes watched the operation to recover the World War II era German Nuclear Bomb. The GPS coordinates Sam had been given—although where and by whom, he refused to divulge—were followed by a team of Navy SEALs and an elite team of bomb disposal experts out of the 832nd Ordnance Battalion US Marine Corps led to an old, rundown, farm property on the outskirts of Virginia.

The property was purchased in 1946 by a man named Reilly Finney—an Alias for Wilhelm Gutwein—and despite being maintained, no one had ever moved onto the farm. On the property the team found an old red tobacco style barn. Despite its dilapidated appearance, a series of modern CCTV surveillance cameras hung surreptitiously from its ceiling and followed their every move.

Inside, the team spaced out and searched the empty barn.

The Secretary depressed the transmitter for her radio. "Check the floor for any access underground."

"Understood, ma'am," came the Marine's reply.

Two minutes later, someone located a hidden trapdoor.

The Secretary felt her heart thumping in her chest. Could it be this easy? Was the threat about to be neutralized? She watched the live video-feed from the Marine's helmet mounted camera. The man opened the trapdoor, revealing a series of steps underground. At the bottom, a large metal door was digitally locked. The door looked like something akin to what you'd find inside a bank's vault. A single SEAL studied the digital pad. It was unlikely anyone was going to guess the code.

The SEAL spoke into his radio, "Madam Secretary, we've hit a snag."

"Understood. We're working on it," the Secretary replied. She turned to Sam Reilly, who was next to the Chairman of the Joint Chiefs of Staff, several military advisers, and the President of the United States. "Mr. Reilly. Did your source mention anything about how to gain access?"

Sam's lips thinned. "I'm sorry. Not a thing."

She turned to the Chairman of the Joint Chiefs of Staff. "How long would it take your team to force entry?"

"Assuming it's not booby-trapped?" He replied with a cocked eyebrow. "It could be hours."

The Secretary smiled. "Or not."

On the live-feed of the door, something suddenly changed. The sound of large, hydraulic locks moving could be heard, and a few seconds later, the security door swung open.

The on-ground team leader ordered everyone out of the barn, while a remote controlled vehicle was sent inside to investigate. The Secretary found herself holding her breath as the remotely operated vehicle made its way down the stairs and into the secure room.

Its overhead LED lights were switched on and its video feed transferred to one of the Command Center's six large display monitors. The RCV made a slow circular sweep of the room. Four large boxes located next to each other in the middle of the room.

The RCV focused its camera in on one of the boxes.

A yellow and black trefoil—the International symbol for nuclear radiation—was plastered all over the box.

The RCV removed the lead cover for the box.

Instantly the Geiger counter started to chirp, indicating the presence of radioactive material. The camera was remotely maneuvered to get a better look.

Inside, were the dismantled components of the German nuclear bomb, and more than a dozen plutonium rods.

The Secretary of Defense sighed heavily. "Thank God. It seems that Wilhelm Gutwein never intended to mount a nuclear attack."

CHAPTER SIXTY-TWO

AFTER THE EXPLOSIONS throughout the capital and along the bridges of the Potomac River, the unidentified army of mercenaries disappeared, seamlessly integrating with other civilians trapped within the city.

An investigation launched immediately afterward discovered that the mercenaries had used the old Dupont Circle underground railway tunnels to escape the barricades and locked down sections of the Capital. The Chairman of the Joint Chiefs of Staff swore he'd hunt them down, and have the perpetrators brought to justice.

The Secretary of Defense interrogated the Chairman of the Joint Chiefs of Staff regarding who authorized the *USS Jimmy Carter* to kidnap Sam Reilly after he dived the *Clarion Call*. She could be quite formidable when the situation required it. In the end, the man had acquiesced and admitted that he was following the advice and intel from a retired senator, named Charles Finney—regarding secrets that were in everyone's interest to be permanently maintained.

She said, "How long have you known the retired Senator Finney?"

"Nearly forty years, ma'am. He's a good man. Helped me get to where I am today. Why do you ask?"

The Secretary tilted her head to the left, and her piercing green eyes fixed on his. "Painter, you weren't involved in this cover up all this time, were you?"

The Chairman of the Joint Chiefs of Staff shook his head. "No ma'am."

Three days after the events that captured the worst nightmares of Americans involving a possible nuclear attack on Washington, D.C., a black SUV drove along K Street. Inside, the Secretary of Defense and Sam Reilly sat silently.

Neither was sure that they wanted to know the truth.

The SUV pulled into the Farrugut Residences.

Sam got out and together with the Secretary of Defense they walked into the main reception area. A small, discreet, security detail followed.

The same stylishly dressed young receptionist met them at the door with a pleasing smile full of teeth.

The Secretary handed over her ID card, and said, "We're here to see retired Senator Charles Finney."

The receptionist's smile faded. "I'm sorry, madam Secretary, but that's not possible."

"Not possible? Did I not make myself clear? This isn't a social visit. We need to see the retired Senator, now."

The young lady swallowed hard and sighed. "I'm sorry, it isn't possible."

"Why not?"

Another woman entered the room, her ID badge showing that she was a registered nurse. "Because he's dead. I'm so sorry, he had a heart attack last night."

"Last night?"

"Yes, it was such a shame. He was such a nice old man."

A forensics team went through the retired Senator Charles Finney's room. Inside, they located an M24 sniper rifle. The ballistics report concluded that the weapon matched the one that killed Congresswoman Bledes.

They also found a safe. Inside, was a single item. A letter from

Werner Heisenberg to the U.S. President Gerald Ford, dated February 1st, 1976. The very day that Heisenberg had died in his own home of kidney and gallbladder cancer.

The Secretary of Defense ran her eyes quickly across the brief letter.

It started with a quote regarding ethics, for which Werner was known to be the author.

> *Where no guiding ideals are left to point the way, the scale of values disappears and with it the meaning of our deeds and sufferings, and at the end can lie only negation and despair. Religion is therefore the foundation of ethics, and ethics the presupposition of life.*

The Secretary blinked, unsure what to make of it.

> *In this, I have tried to do what I believe is right for my fellow man, but in this endeavor and through all the good intentions in the world, I fear I may have unleashed the worst of mankind's intrinsic failings – that of greed.*

The Secretary read quickly over the next part, pausing on the end of the letter.

> *I believe that nuclear fission is too great a Genie for any one nation to behold and that possibly such power could be shared between a few nations – what I had hoped to be the United Nations – in an endeavor to create perpetual peace on Earth.*
>
> *In the effort, I believe I have failed. I now share with you a list of names and persons involved in one of the greatest deceits ever to take place, and pray that you may find it within your power to rectify what I could not.*

The Secretary skimmed the names. She'd already heard them all before.

At the end of the document, it was signed,

Werner Heisenberg

CHAPTER SIXTY-THREE

U.N. HEADQUARTERS, NEW YORK

NEARLY EVERY SEAT within the U.N. General Assembly hall was occupied. A hundred-and-ninety-three-member countries were seated in alphabetical order throughout the amphitheater, including the five permanent members of the Security Council: China, France, Russia, United Kingdom, and United States—all allies during World War II, and nuclear weapons states.

Congressman Peter Grzonkowski looked tired. He had been answering questions for an hour and forty-five minutes. The Chairman of the United Nations asked if the witness considering recent terrorist events in Washington D.C., wanted a short recess.

The Congressman shook his head. "No, sir. I'm ready to conclude." Shoulders back, he sat up straight, so he could speak clearly into the microphone at the front of his desk. "In the morning of August 6, 1945," he said, "the world changed forever when the *Enola Gay* dropped the first nuclear weapon on the Japanese city of Hiroshima."

There was a lingering silence within the General Assembly. Nearly eight decades had passed, but memory of the horrific event came vividly to everyone's mind.

Grzonkowski continued, "For the first time in history, we developed the power to destroy not just each other, but our entire species, through nuclear war." He paused to let that concept sit there for a moment. "This was an evolutionary achievement that no other creature on earth had attained."

His eyes swept the silent faces of those who filled the amphitheater. "It has been long considered that the innovation of the atomic bomb brought about a new era of peace, unseen in any other stage of humanity's existence."

Congressman Grzonkowski took a sip of water from the glass in front of him and swallowed. "Historians argue that the physicist Robert Oppenheimer, should have been given a Nobel Peace Prize for his work toward the development of a nuclear bomb. As I explained previously, that title should have gone to all four men involved in its propagation."

He closed his eyes and took a deep breath. "In 1947 a German Physicist named Werner Heisenberg realized that the atom bomb was not enough to ensure peace now that the human race had the ability to destroy the entire world."

Grzonkowski opened his eyes again. "Heisenberg felt there should be an opposing superpower, like two sides of the Earth's magnetic poles, to maintain balance through nuclear deterrence. With this in mind, he gave the Soviet Union the key to the Genie, and the Soviet Atomic Bomb Project was born.

"Thus, the Cold War began.

"Yet wars, even cold wars, need fuel," Grzonkowski said. "A World War II hero, Charles Finney, a good friend of the then United States Secretary of Defense, James Forrestal, launched a clandestine plan. His idea was to promote perpetual war, and accordingly, from his point of view, obtain peace.

"Finney utilized the benefit of a young shipping owner, named Michael Reilly, to sell weapons grade uranium and armaments to the Soviet Union.

"Meanwhile, backed by a select group of people within the United States, Charles Finney continued to promote Cold War propaganda and the doctrine of Mutually Assured Destruction. Powerful men became richer, while dissidents were silenced to ensure this secret remained forever hidden.

"Finney believed that humanity needed the ongoing threat of nuclear destruction.

"Yet with the development of the internet, free trade, and the global market, it's not just nuclear threat that makes war unviable– its economics. Commerce is a game that everyone can win. We must make the price of war too expensive and the rewards too paltry. We need opposing superpowers to work together in financial trade.

"While the media would have you believe differently, deaths through war has been in decline since 1945. Today, despite Syria and Iraq, we are not anywhere near the levels seen during the Chinese Civil War, Korea, Vietnam, India/Pakistan/Bangladesh, Iran-Iraq, USSR-Afghanistan, and many regions of Africa.

"As a species, we've come together. I think it's time we address the possibility of a world without nuclear bombs. Has there been peace because of the nuclear deterrent, or because we have evolved?

"Today, we are living in the most nonviolent era in the existence of our species. I believe, in the not too distant future, the threat of Mutually Assured Destruction will not be necessary. Although Heisenberg was ahead of his time, there was one thing he got wrong, something he never could have predicted back in 1947. Something that would inevitably change the course of human evolution."

Grzonkowski paused. "The innovation and rise of the Internet."

He exhaled a deep breath. "This led to a world of globalization unimaginable back in 1947, where all countries are connected through communication and trade, rendering the price of war too expensive, and the rewards too meager. No one wants to harm their customers.

"Given time, I believe nuclear weapons will disarm, and the human race, having risen far from its humble beginnings as hunter gatherers, will finally enjoy peace on earth."

THE END

WANT MORE?

Join my email list and get a FREE and EXCLUSIVE Sam Reilly story that's not available anywhere else!

Join here ~ www.bit.ly/ChristopherCartwright

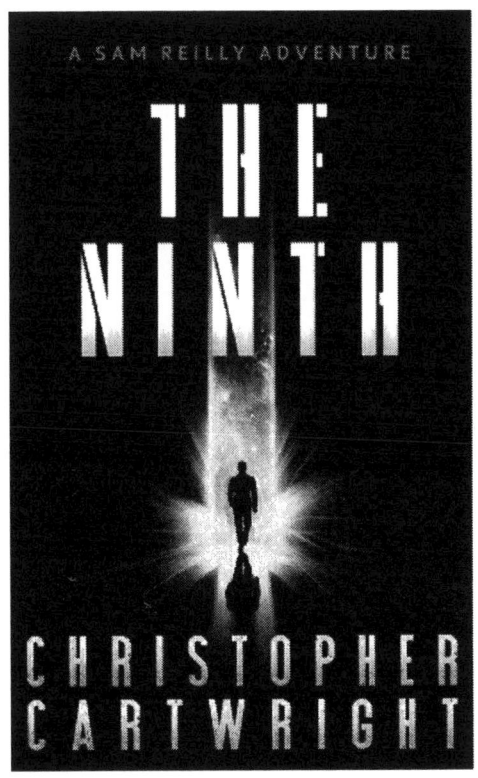

Printed in Great Britain
by Amazon